THE INTERVIEW

Hope this is a delight to read...

THE INTERVIEW

MUKUL KUNDRA

PAPER TOWNS
PUBLISHERS

First published by
Papertowns Publishers
72, Vishwanath Dham Colony,
Niwaru Road, Jhotwara,
Jaipur, 302012

The Interview

ISBN Print Book - 978-93-94670-07-5

Illustration by Gopika
Insta Handle: __g.o.p.i.k.a__

Printed in India

For my beloved Grandparents,
Late Om Prakash Kundra
And
Late Darshana Rani Kundra

Acknowledgement

A relatable story enables one to find a different perspective on life and its struggles. This idea stuck with me while I wrote this story. It took me more than a year to pen it down, but my firm belief in the idea made me consistent. In my mind, I lived the life of the protagonist, all this while. Now when it has reached completion, it seems as though I have met each character in real life. This journey wasn't a straight line, and thus, I am deeply grateful to all people, and of course, Vihaan, who were a part of it.

I would like to express my sincere gratitude to my parents for their immense support. My siblings; Rishab, Ishita, Yashvi, Akshit, and Manya for their belief in me. There were times when I faced challenges in carrying my story forward, but my uncles, Pankaj & Lalit helped me in overcoming every obstacle to bring out the best in this book.

Special thanks to Paragi Neema, who helped me in the completion of the plot, and for her advise and assistance in editing this work. Without her support, this project would not have reached to this stage.

Also, a big thanks to my bhabhi, Neha, and my friend, Abhinav, who motivated me to start writing this novel after I took a long break from writing.

Thanks to all my school and college buddies who were always beside me, inspiring to write this book.

My first two books, "Friendship: A Puzzle to Solve" and "How Old Are You" were a great success. Not only was I able to sell more than 5000 copies in total, but I also received immense love from the readers.

My deepest gratitude to all the other people who were a part of my journey that I couldn't thank here personally due to paucity of space. That doesn't lessen my gratitude for them. I do not want to forget people who were always there for me, contributing to my happiness and success.

I hope you enjoy reading this...

I broke the silence and said "I am not committing suicide, stay calm guys. I would have done it earlier if I had to."

"Ek baat sahi hai yahan
Manzil na mili toh chaaro taraf khaai hai
Neechay dekhta hu toh kankaal nazar aatay hai
Shayad unko bhi manzil nahi mili…."

I took a bus to Varanasi but didn't go home, my destination was different…

Content

"One day, you think you have all the time in the world; the next, you wake up and wonder what you should do with it."

Chapter 1

Referral

As per the society's decade old norm, I should have not commenced my Sunday morning until 10'o'clock or so, but I woke up at 5 am, an hour before the alarm was supposed to set off. Erratic behaviour indeed by the normal standards. I was able to hear the Gayatri mantra chanted in a chorus, and for the last 50 days, it had served well for me as an alarm.

"Om bhūr bhuvaḥ svaḥ
tat savitur vareṇyaṃ
bhargo devasya dhīmahi
dhiyo yo naḥ prachodayāt………"

Waking up to the Gayatri mantra had become my daily routine. Backed up by scientific evidence, regular chanting of the Gayatri Mantra elevates one's concentration, and its regular recitation is also capable of acting as an effective anti-toxin for the mind and body of an individual. However, it didn't have the slightest impact on me. After all, I had a perpetual determination backed by the intention to achieve my goal, and my mind would find some peace only when the same is transmuted into reality. For the last 50 days, I had the purest desire to get a chance to prove myself, but not even once did I get an opportunity. Averting my thoughts, I quickly took a bath, dressed up well, and made my way into the same building where I was facing daily rejections. As it was a daily routine, I went up to the reception and politely sought approval for them to allow me to meet the head of their management, in entirety for once, and also conveyed the fact that I will be patiently waiting outside the building the whole day. I sought but only one chance.

It was around 12 noon, and similar to how other days went, I was rapidly losing any hope of receiving an opportunity, but to my utmost surprise, I saw someone approaching me. He was a decently dressed, tall, broad-shouldered gentleman with his beard furnishing evidence of wisdom. I had never encountered him before and took him to be a random visitor.

"Hello, son, what are you doing here?" he asked me with a gentle tone.

"Ahh...hi sir, I have requested an appointment with the director of operations of the establishment and I am looking forward to my turn," I replied.

"Why do you want to be here? I am of the opinion that you are not eligible," he told me.

"I was here a few days ago but I failed to fulfil their expectations and was asked to leave. Now, I come here every day with the sheer hope I might get another chance.

I am of the strong opinion that everyone deserves that, right?" I questioned.

"I don't think you belong here if you failed once. You should move on from here, my son. Don't waste your life waiting here," he said while trying to alter my current intention with his one hand on my shoulder.

"For the first time in my life, and in entirety, I am absolutely determined about something, and I will achieve it one day no matter what. It is my 51st day waiting outside the building, and I will come here daily till I get a chance to prove myself," I replied without a strand of doubt.

"Oh, okay, if that's the case, would you mind if I take your interview? I may attempt to refer you after all."

I agreed without hesitation of any form or kind.

He continued, "I have but one condition. If you were to fail in convincing me, then you will do whatever I direct you to, without any further queries. Tomorrow morning at 9 a.m., you are invited to my residence. I hope to see you there and you may want to be well prepared", succeeding his dialogue, the gentleman wrote down his address on a piece of paper which he then shared with me, gave me his blessings, and departed from the venue.

I had about 20 hours or so to prepare myself for the upcoming interview session and I was certainly not going to fail yet again, under any and all circumstances. I plunged into the preparation without any further delay. Under ordinary circumstances, one may leverage the internet known to the common person for most of the interview preparations, but for this particular interview, every source may prove to be useless. In those 20 hours, I drafted every possible question and ensured that I strategized my answers for the same. While it is often easy to prepare a good answer in your head, its articulation, and delivery in reality are what pose a challenge. So, I had to work on eloquence. As the deadline approached, my mind started going off track and I found myself constantly altering my preparation goals. With time, I realised that the suite of answers I had at my disposal at the moment would not suffice and that I needed more time to polish the same.

The next day, I got up at 6 in the morning and prepared physically and mentally for the interview. I checked my sleep cycle in my fitness band. It was what one may call truly erratic, 3 hours 24 minutes of sleep and out of that only 1 hour 2 minutes of deep sleep. The Fitbit app suggested that I should sleep for a couple of hours more for better health. I could feel the fatigue hitting me, yet I somehow felt energetic at the same time. After having excessive coffee, I packed my bag, and left home. I usually travel by bus as it keeps a constructive check on my budget, but today I was not willing to favour the probability for any risk. I reached the deemed destination an hour before the interview was scheduled. Standing outside the gentleman's house, I saw him come out to receive the morning newspaper, but strangely he ignored me at the moment.

At 8:58 a.m., I rang his doorbell and nervously rubbed my palms together. He opened the door exactly at 9 a.m., and in those two minutes, millions of thoughts crossed my mind, out of which only 2 or 3 were relevant.

"Good morning, son! You arrived ahead of time, as I expected," he said while guiding me towards the room. Without paying my greetings, I followed the path he directed and hence, I have reasons to believe that I didn't make a positive impression.

"I know you haven't had your breakfast today. We shall proceed once you have it. My servant is preparing the same at the moment," he said and left the room.

After 5 minutes, his servant entered the room and served me the meal. I wasn't hungry and the feeling of nausea held a tight grip on me because of the nervousness, but I finished my breakfast to offer a good impression about myself. It was the first time in my life that I finished everything that was served on my plate.

I picked the plate and went out to the kitchen while being unsure of the right path. The house wasn't that big after all. Later, the servant came in and politely asked me to accompany him to the study. It was a room perfect for a bibliophile.

"Come and have a seat," the gentleman spoke politely as I entered the room.

"I am sorry I didn't ask your name," he said

"Sir, my name is Vihaan Miglani. I am from Varanasi, and have pursued…" I replied, to which he interrupted me while quoting, "I just asked your name. Don't be in a hurry. We have enough time so you can tell everything about yourself as we begin."

"So, Vihaan, you have already been given 15 days to complete the task, right?" he asked.

"Yes, sir. They gave me 15 days as per the rules" I agreed.

"So, like everyone else, you got your chance and you failed to achieve what you intended to. So, give me one reason why I should recommend you?" he exclaimed.

I got nervous as I was expecting some fundamental queries initially, but instead, he directly marked the inception of the questionnaire from the primary point. With the will to furnish true clarity, I replied, "Sir, I have encountered a lot in my life as we speak, and now this remains as the only option I have to continue further."

He started laughing and paused to ask with an expression of surprise "I think you are only 21-22 years old if I am not wrong, and at this age you have faced a lot!? Are you trying to gain sympathy from me?"

"No, I don't want your sympathy. I am certain you will offer me a second chance after you are done listening to my story," I replied with an expression of unshaken confidence.

"Are you sure, Vihaan? I am generally not convinced easily," he followed my reply with an immediate query.

"Yes sir, I am sure but you will have to listen to the whole story. It might be a bit long so I hope you have enough time for that."

"Okay, please go ahead and explain yourself. You can take as much time as you want and I promise I will not end this interview till you complete your part. I am all ears."

I got excited and opened my bag taking out all my diaries before commencing the story.

"Why are you taking out all these diaries?" he asked with an element of surprise on his face.

"Sir, I don't intend to miss anything. I have recorded the elements of my entire life by means of these diaries being a part of the dossier that represent me essentially. It is the first time that someone is willing to listen to my story and hence, I want to make sure to narrate all the parts and connected events that led me here," I responded with my eyes gleaming with enthusiasm and sorrow at the same time.

"I have divided my story into sets of different chapters. I shall start from the very beginning and if you have any queries, I would request you to put them forward after I mark the conclusion of that part." The instructions were put forward by me with a feeling of ecstasy.

I took a long, deep breath and started with the first chapter....

"Life offers two paths: one leads to chaos, the other to JEE prep. Let's just say, JEE prep is the ultimate test."

Chapter 2

Demand Draft

A lady standing in front of the desk exclaimed with an eerie look, "Last one hour left, hurry up!" The apparent feeling was like someone had deployed a time constraint bomb. My pulse rate was off the charts, way beyond the normal standards. I rushed through the question paper in haste, rolling my eyes over each question out there. I placed my pencil on the desk and looked across the room. Every student in the room seemed like a lifeless zombie, hardly blinking their eyes. Some were pretending to solve the questions and the rest were solving the same with confidence. I promptly closed my eyes and tried recalling the inception of my journey to this room with the intention to calm my senses, but to no good. I could feel the question paper laughing at me and all of a sudden, the watch in that room started ringing. I woke up instantly, feeling my heart throbbing in my throat and the rate of transpiration for my body was at the maximum as well. I could feel chills going down the spine at regular intervals. I picked up my phone and checked the time, it displayed 4:30 AM. I took a long breath, "It was just a bad dream, I should relax." I calibrated my body, leveraging the feeling of ecstasy, went to the kitchen for a glass of water intending to hydrate, and then made my way to the balcony. The surroundings were pitch black, the street lights were off and the only sound I could hear was that of an air conditioner.

I picked my chemistry book off the shelf and switched on my study lamp. Flipping through the pages of the book, I could not help but think about the dream. It was 6:00 a.m. already and my mother noticed the light in my room from the narrow recess beneath the door. She entered and saw me sleeping on my book with some pages wet from the drooling of saliva.

"Vihaan, are you fine?" Mom asked.

"Yes, mom, I was just revising and refreshing my memory for some topics," I answered.

"I think you should go and sleep for now. You have been working relentlessly for quite some time now. It is time to give your body the rest it deserves and requires," she suggested.

My mind was numb, and as a generic machine who obeys the commands and instructions of the issuer, I fulfilled the same. My eyes were only partially open and everything around me seemed blurred. My journey from my study table to my bed took a moment or so and my eyes were completely shut as I entered the world of my dreams in a split second. All this while, my eyes opened for a moment and I was back in the world of my dreams.

I was able to hear the distinct sound of the birds chirping, the screeching noise of the furniture in motion and the whistle of a pressure cooker. It was 9 o'clock in the morning and everyone was in an overwhelming hurry since they were late for work as usual. I went to the washroom to freshen up and sat at the dining table for breakfast. My mom served me an omelette accompanied by a cup of milk. I was revising the periodic table and some key concepts from physics while having the meal. With the exams approaching 10 days later, I had no time to eat patiently. I got ready physically and mentally to leave for the extra class at Science Coaching Pvt. Ltd. I believe it was after 30 classes or so that I was so attentive in the class after all. I was confused whether this was a direct result of the recent dream that I had or the fact that the exams were approaching. And like every other science student, I had, on an average, invested 16-18 hours a day into studying and put a halt on every fun activity that a school student can potentially and possibly have.

"Class, today is our last session before the entrance exam, and your Chemistry and Mathematics teachers intend to have a word with you." The Physics mentor announced.

It may be quoted as a classical example for déjà vu as something similar had happened right before the 12th board exams.

The Physics mentor wrote "JEE MAINS" with bold text formatting on the whiteboard and then proceeded to call the other two teachers.

I was engaged in the activity of placing all my books inside the bag when my Physics mentor pointed, "Vihaan, you may do it later, please pay attention here for now."

"So, students, you all have worked hard and we all are proud of you. When you all joined our institute, we were doubtful, but now it seems that all of you can crack the entrance exam easily. Our staff and teachers have done their part. It is now time to show your true potential to the wild world out there."

We all certainly could experience goosebumps and chills as we heard the speech, and we were both excited and filled with an eerie feeling at the same moment. They continued their motivational speech for the next 15 minutes or so. The first two minutes were really interesting but later, it came across as any other boring speech that we used to hear by our school principal during the morning assembly. In the end, they showed us the poster of a boy who got AIR 57 and said, "Now it's your turn to be there in this frame." It was the same photo they showed me two years ago when I had come to their institute for admission. I ignored the part and picked my bag with the subtle intention to rush back home.

I chalked out an efficient plan of action for the revision session by organizing the chapters and the relevant subjects based on the projected marks that each carried, and stuck it on my cupboard. Apparently, the days were passing at a moment's notice and the day of verdict was approaching with time. Yes, "verdict", since all our efforts in general and lives in particular, were going to be judged based on the entrance exam.

Before anyone realised, the remaining number of days left literally changed to hours. 36 hours before the exam, to be precise, I decided to not study and indulge in other activities of all forms and kinds with the intention to relax my mind. But somewhere within, the inner folds of my mind were putting up a strong recommendation for one final revision. There was a constant conflict between my brain and heart. My books filled the position of drugs at that moment. I needed them around myself at any point in time and was going through a similar feeling as a full-blown addict.

On the final day before the examination, I decided to sleep early, and before retiring off to sleep, I called my friends to wish them good luck. That night was a long one, perhaps the longest in quite a while. Millions of thoughts crossed my mind and amongst those thoughts, was the recollection of the Gauss theorem. I was rechecking my bag, repeatedly. I was checking my pencil box, admit card and of course my token of good luck. Next day, I woke up quite early in the morning and prepared for the set of events to come. The only thing I had for breakfast was a bowl of curd with sugar, a common practice backed by the belief that it is supposed to bring good luck for the day. My father took a leave from his office that very day since he wanted to be with me. I requested blessings from my mother and grandparents and went outside while my father was struggling to start off the engine of his old scooter. We are a lower middle-class family that has a small house and a dream to buy a car one day. After 3-4 hits and trials, the scooter started. The journey from my home to the examination venue was a very peaceful one with a refreshing cold breeze rushing against my face, capable of relieving me of all of my worries for the moment.

When I finally reached the destination, I saw thousands of students accompanied by their parents and in a nervous stance and engaged in the thought about the examination result even before appearing for it. We rushed into the building as the guard opened the gate.

“All the best. Give your best, my son,” my father shouted from afar. I was heavily vested in my own thoughts and didn’t turn my back.

In accordance with my earlier dream, I was allocated the first seat which immediately filled me with an eerie feeling but somehow, I tried to calm myself down. They handed out one form to fill out before the test began as a part of the necessary documentation. That form, as I believe, was more difficult to complete as compared to the entrance examination.

The question paper and OMR sheet were distributed thereafter but we were not allowed to open it, just yet. A bell rang, marking the inception of the examination and the invigilator asked us thereafter to proceed ahead as well. It was like a race to open the paper first. My plan was to analyse the questions as I solved them, one at a time, starting from the subject physics, and decided to make my way to the OMR sheet to mark the answers towards the end.

Questions were not as difficult as I expected and I managed to wrap up the examination in entirety, within 2 hours and 30 minutes. I had 30 minutes to fill the OMR but I am not certain what struck me. I started solving the questions I left for later.

I didn't realize that the exam was about to get over and only 10 minutes were left when I started filling OMR. My heart was throbbing beyond the normal cardiac cycle and my palms were heavily sweating as well. In a haste, I committed errors in 5 answers inside the OMR. I was disappointed at my impatience but in reality, the rest of the paper went fine.

When I came out of the examination venue, I saw my father standing with a group of people that seemed to be comprise the parents of students who were discussing the syllabus.

"How did it go? It went well, right?" my father asked.

"Yes, papa, it was good. I just marked some wrong answers towards the end since I panicked a little," I replied.

"Don't worry, you will clear it. You must be hungry, let us go and have something," my father said.

For lunch, he took me to a nearby restaurant. I believe that was my first visit to a diner. My father ordered one platter for me and a glass of water for himself.

"Aren't you hungry, dad?" I asked.

"No, Vihaan, I had my lunch outside the center," he responded.

I could, with little effort, realise that he was lying to me because he didn't have any money left. I intentionally ate only half of the platter and asked him to either have the remaining half or get it vaulted and packed up. It took but a few minutes for him to finish the same which reflected his hunger.

After lunch, I went to the coaching center to have an estimate for both my score and the rank. According to the answer key that my institute released, I will get at least 152 marks. The rank prediction was tough as the 12th standard board examination results had a remarkable 40% influence on the final rank and the same was yet to be announced.

I planned a day out with the family with the intention to unwind and relax for at least two days but waiting for the result demanded more patience than studying for the examination itself and whenever I tried relieving my memories about the same, someone took the opportunity, without delay to remind me of it by asking how the examination went. Apart from that, every other institute had published its answer key and I calculated my score using each of them. According to one, the projected score is 190 while the other furnished 110. Sooner, rather than later, I realized they didn't serve any good except making me feel overwhelmed for no reason since reality is indeed what matters.

To be very honest, the night before the day of result was not as frightening as I expected it to be, and that made me sleep quite peacefully.

"Vihaan, JEE Mains result is out. This year's cut-off is 95," my father said while waking me up.

Without any further ado, I ran to the nearby cybercafé with my admit card. About 10-12 students were already waiting in a queue for their turn.

"Tell me your roll no. and centre number," a boy sitting on the front desk asked.

I was startled for a moment but caught my senses immediately thereafter, "456002, and the centre number is 2236," I replied.

"Your score is 83, you are not qualified," he said.

I was suffocating, felt breathlessness as if someone had plugged my nostrils.

"Don't cry, Chetan," he exclaimed.

I wiped my nose and said "My name is not Chetan. I am Vihaan, Vihaan Miglani."

"But it shows Chetan Kaushik. Look at the screen," he replied.

I glared across to the screen with blurry eyes, wiped my tears and read through it. I checked the roll number and found that he had entered the same incorrectly. I shared my roll number with him again and now the correct result card appeared.

"I am sorry, your score is 178 and your rank is 22,000," he responded.

I checked my result several times for the sake of confirmation and once done, I should have been smiling but instead, I started crying again.

I took out a printout for the result published and rushed towards home. I was taken aback to see the crowd gathered outside my home accompanied by an ambulance. I rushed my way towards the entrance of the house and discovered that they were taking my father on a stretcher with an oxygen mask on his face. I rushed to sit in the ambulance beside him. My mind was totally blank and I was simply able to see him struggling for each breath by the passing moments.

Doctors took him to the emergency ward and commenced the analysis followed by the treatment. There was some transparent disturbance in the ward and I got more tense as I saw the same.

"We have to shift him to the ICU immediately. He had a heart attack. Could you please fill this form and deposit one lakh rupees?" the doctor informed me.

While the elders in my family were busy dealing with the situation with highest priority, I started to think how my life was so similar to that of Raju in 3 Idiots- financially stuck and father critically ill, but the line was drawn at the fact that unlike Raju, I didn't even have the other two idiots in my life.

My father's condition improved after 36 hours and I went to his room all excited to share the result of my examination. The news filled him up with joy up to the brim and we both shared a momentary feeling of mutual happiness.

As I was leaving the room, my father spoke softly, "Vihaan, come back" I made my way back in order to verify if everything was fine.

"I haven't seen your mom, if she is outside, then tell her to see me" my father asked me.

"Yes, dad, she is mustering all her patience and is currently in the waiting room, scared to see you in the current state", I replied.

My father gave out an intense laugh and said, "Tell her I am alive and well and I am now in a condition to tease her."

I made my way to the waiting room and politely asked my mother to meet dad. While the love birds were preoccupied with their conversation, I stood outside the room with an attempt to eavesdrop. My ears caught attention when their conversation digressed from the primary topic towards the hospital expenditure. I could sense the atmosphere became a bit tense. The expenses exceeded our family's budget. I heard my father saying that he had saved to the last penny for my college fees.

I got a bit emotional, and anxious, too. Will this obstacle prevent me from attending my dream college? How will my parents bear the tuition expenses? Multiple thoughts crossed my conscious mind. I saw a guy with a laptop in the waiting room and politely asked if I could use it for a moment or so. Generously, he gave me his laptop without asking any further queries. My fingers moved swiftly as I typed with the intention to discover the fees of IITs and other Universities. I was exposed to reality in a jiffy. The fees that we were looking at for an IIT was way too high and it demotivated me to appear for the JEE Advanced exam.

My father was supposed to rest for at least 10 days but we were limited by our financial condition. Things got back to what one may call "normal" and days started passing like moments yet again. I wasn't very stressed about the exam because somewhere down, I knew we won't be able to afford IIT irrespective of the result, and hence, I had nothing to lose. The exam duration was 3 hours each for

2 different sections of the paper. The exam wasn't exactly challenging for me since I was able to solve the questions with ease. I was certain I would clear the examination after I finished the same.

"Vihaan, how was your exam?" My father asked.

"I gave my best but there are really few chances that I will clear it," I shared with hesitation.

Lying to my parents wasn't a habit of mine. But this lie was for our family's greater good and I then left everything to my destiny and God.

Few days later, the day commenced with a usual morning for me, a sort of Déjà vu as my father woke me up and I rushed again to the cybercafé with the admit card in my hand. I secured 2034 rank in JEE advance. It was enough to make my way into some IIT. While walking from the cybercafé to my residence, I was just wholeheartedly praying to God that my dad should be fine because things were repeating, and I didn't want that incident to happen again.

"Dad, I have got an All-India Rank of 17,400," I lied to my father.

"So, is it good news or bad one? Will you be able to get admission into an IIT?" my dad asked.

"I have cleared the exam but I will not be able to make it to any IIT as we are from the General category. Also, I have checked about the admission on the internet and will be able to secure a seat in some Delhi college," I responded.

He got worried as I couldn't make it to his dream college. He might not know the fundamentals about engineering but like every other father of a science student, it was his dream college. Not for himself, but for me, to be precise.

"Don't worry, dad. Delhi Imperial College is just like an IIT, and I might even secure a full-time scholarship there," I tried to console him.

"Okay, Vihaan, if you say so. Just let me know the college fees," my father said and went inside his room.

A calculator and passbook accompanied him to his room. He was calculating the money he would require in addition to his savings.

Next day, I woke up at 9:30 a.m. and was introduced to the fact that my father had left already. I opened my cupboard to take out my clothes and I found that my admit card was missing. I searched for it everywhere while using my Sherlock brain. The only thing I was able to find was a bank statement. I opened it and saw the account balance. Rs. 54,000/- was written at the last page of the statement. It was Rs. 25,000 less than the fees of the college I was planning to go to.

Just when I was about to keep it back at its place, I heard some noise. Someone was sobbing nearby. I followed the sound and it took me towards the room which was supposed to be locked. It was my grandparents' room. It was the scariest room in my house as it was full of old stuff and dusty furniture. Although I was too little to remember anything about them and had only seen them in a photo frame, I always had a feeling of their presence inside the room as if they were still the residents of the same.

I opened the dark room and saw a person sitting on the chair. I knew he was my father, I switched on the lights and said, “Dad, why are you in this room? What happened? Why are you crying, is everything fine?”

“Don’t talk to me, Vihaan. Just leave the room.” My dad answered sadly.

“But dad, why are you crying?” I replied.

“I thought that we both shared a good bond and were supposed to share each and everything. Today, I am really disappointed,” he said.

I didn’t know what he was trying to say. It was as though he had heard some news about me having a pregnant girlfriend or that I had started taking drugs. I hadn’t done anything at all except having books as my only girlfriend. I pulled myself out of my thoughts back into the realm of reality and focused my brain towards the task of high urgency at hand. I was here to devise the necessary action required to resolve the situation, not mock it.

“I haven’t done anything wrong, dad, and will never do anything that disappoints you,” I replied and put my hands on his shoulder.

“Why did you lie to me about your result?” my father exclaimed with the tone that puts across a query.

“I…I….” I stammered.

"I want to know the reason, Vihaan," my father asked again.

"That day in the hospital, I heard you and mom talk about the financial issues and I realized that the fees at IIT is way too high. You have done a lot for me and I don't want to be a burden on you." I answered.

He hugged me emotionally. I went out of the house to buy some latest movie DVDs from a nearby store. Most of all, I was excited about my upcoming college life after 2 months and the adventures that awaited me. I couldn't contain my curiosity to experience college, friends, trips, parties, and everything that college life encompasses or had to offer.

'3 idiots' was one of my favourite titles. I watched one movie after the other, all based on lifelong friendships made in college, and after 24 hours of binge watching, I started relating my life with Bollywood movies. As an implication of watching all those movies, I was silly enough to conclude that a group of 3 friends is the best to have, but presently I had none.

I spent the remaining days doing things and performing tasks which I had earlier stopped indulging myself in due to examinations, such as sports. Apart from that, I used to go for a holy bath in Ganga daily in the morning. I hailed from a small town; Varanasi, which was only small in terms of land area.

While logically, and in reality, there are only 24 hours in each day, apparently the hours equate to 48 when you don't have any significant work to do. It was indeed the same with me. After having fun for the first few days, I actually missed those hardworking days when my life only revolved around studies. I wanted to get busy and somehow be able to relive them. In a short moment, I erased the wish to go back to the past as I very well knew that my brain would actually have to suffer again. I wanted to gain some new skills during this time period but was too lazy to even pick up a pen. I just wanted to relax and do nothing.

Like the majority of other nations that existed on the planet, India is also moving rapidly towards digitalisation, and hence, the admission procedure was purely online. Due to lack of resources, I had to pay a visit to the cybercafé for every computer related and relevant task. I went to the cybercafe and carefully noted all the details and documents required for admission, 10 days before the event was scheduled to begin. There were two things which were primarily required to be arranged- money towards the initial fee payment, and for the tickets, so that we could travel to Delhi for submission of documents after the selection procedure was over. For us, the sum required for the tickets was not a big concern. The main issue at hand was the college fee as the present bank balance was insufficient. Loan approval in such a short duration of time was not an option as well, so my father went to his boss, friends and his relatives to arrange it. However, we didn't receive any help but excuses from anyone and everyone.

"Dad, were you able to arrange the primary sum of money required?" I asked.

"Yes, Vihaan, I have arranged some, and in 2-3 days I will be able to arrange the complete sum," my father replied.

With around 5-6 piggy banks in our house, my parents broke them one by one to gather the amount but it summed up to the cost of a train ticket only. My father's usual working hours were from 10am-6pm, but in those days he used to leave the house by 8 or 8:30 in the morning and come back by 8 or 9 in the evening. He was steaming himself to the maximum from one place to another with the intention to make the required sum. For an upper middle-class family, Rs. 25,000 is certainly not a lot, but for us it meant sacrificing our sleep to fulfil our aspirations. Days were passing by without any financial progress of any form or kind, and being a child, I was not permitted to worry on this front. In India, people believe that children are not required to concern themselves or interfere in financial issues or matters and all problems belong to parents and family. We are expected to just relax and concentrate only on studies. I was wondering what I should be concentrating on. I didn't have anything to do at present.

"Dad, I think I might not be able to join college this year, so I think I should start preparing for next year." I got the statement across with a high temperament.

My dad didn't say a word at that time but he was broken by my words. As an Indian dad, he wasn't expected to expose his weak side to his son. Although consumed by anger at the way I spoke to my father, my mom did not scold me because somewhere down, even she was concerned about my career.

In a small town, getting a loan from a bank is really tough, so people with surplus funds run their business in the finance niche. They give money on interest by considering property, vehicles, gold, etc as collateral. Their interest rate is nearly double as compared to the bank because it is a privately held business and also has its advantages, the primary one being that the loan service is easy and accessible.

My dad declared a property as collateral to get some money at an interest rate of 14% per annum. I was unaware of the fact and when he told me that he had arranged the money, he became my superhero at that very moment. The journey of my dad becoming the villain of my career to a superhero only took a day and I ensured he received my gratitude by touching his feet and requesting his blessings.

We packed our bags and left for the capital of Delhi. Before we left, my mom did a small prayer and added sweeteners to our mouth in the form of curd and sugar to ensure, in her good opinion, that we had a safe and successful journey. It was the first time I was travelling out of town. I tried enacting like Hrithik Roshan from ZNMD, truly feeling the ambience in terms of the wind blowing through my hair with my head hanging off the train window in free air. While doing it, I got a reality check from my father that my hand or head can suffer a fatal blow due to any obstacle in the way. Immediately thereafter, I snapped back to real life and went to the upper berth to sleep for a while. I could hardly sleep even for an hour because of the feeling of true ecstasy. Like every engineering aspirant, I wanted to be in IIT and was lucky enough to be eligible, but my destiny had something else in hold for me and for some reason I was not sad about it.

I was half asleep when I heard a train whistle being blown up and people yelling and screaming at each other- “Get aside”, “Pick your luggage”, etc. My father woke me up and asked me to wear my shoes as we were about to reach Delhi railway station within the next few minutes. I was startled to see such a huge crowd at the railway station. The number of people I was introduced to at the station was equal if not more than the number of people that reside in my town. We were also surrounded by some people wearing red clothes. They were there to pick luggage. That atmosphere pumped my body and mind with excitement and raised my level of joy even further. We took an auto rickshaw from outside which charged us double as compared to the standard price just because we were new to that city. As soon as we checked into a guest house, my father called and informed my mother that we had arrived safely. The guest house was quite expensive for us, but the cheapest in Delhi.

"Vihaan, now go and take a quality rest for some time. Then, we can visit a few places in Delhi and post confirmation for your admission, we will leave for home. Also, check all your documents at once," my father advised.

I was preoccupied with the excitement to leave to an extent that I forgot to vet all my documents. I took my bag that housed the essentials like water and some snacks that my mom had packed for us since Delhi is an expensive city.

Delhi stands as a well-known city for everyone in India even if they have visited it or not. We went to see a few significant places such as the India gate, Red Fort & Chandni Chowk (paradise of street food). We had our lunch from the roadside vendors, because in restaurants, drinking water was also chargeable.

City tour was quite along the lines of my dream but the next day was the most important. I got up at 6 a.m. in the morning and we left the guest house by 7 or so because the college campus, which was our primary destination, was 20-22km away. We reached 30 minutes before the registration started. The entrance gate was quite similar to the college gate in 3 idiots. The gate was black in colour and it was about 20-30 feet tall and in front of the gate stood two guards with a uniform and a wooden stick in their hands. They saluted us as we entered the campus. As soon as we crossed the main door there was a board that welcomed us and the venue for registration was explicitly mentioned and labelled as "Auditorium". We politely asked the guard to direct the way towards that hall.

"Excuse me, where is this auditorium? I am here for the admission," I exclaimed.

"Take left from that round about and then take the first right," the guard answered.

First left was 400 m far but the right turn was so far that it took 15 minutes to reach there by walking. Apparently, it was not a college but a small educational town indeed. On the way to the auditorium, we encountered some monkeys & peacocks as well.

My imagination insisted that the hall would have a window and we would have to stand in a queue for admission like we did while purchasing the railway tickets from the station, but in reality, it was totally different. The auditorium had a seating of 2500 people and a lobby which was 10 times the size of my house if I am not wrong. Gate was like that of a movie theatre and equally heavy to open.

As I opened it, I saw some officials sitting on a centre stage with formal dress code and one lady was requesting us to sit as the process was delayed by 30 minutes due to some technical error already. Seats were of much higher quality than the seats of the movie theatre in our town. Usually, government buildings do not smell the best and look old and weary but the infrastructure at the government colleges seem to be better than private colleges.

I was knitting my custom world of imagination, extrapolating my thoughts about the rest of campus, when suddenly the lady announced that everyone would have to come and take the form and attach all the documents in a file in order to do the needful. My father asked me to rush and take that form before anyone else. I procured the form, filled the same, it was a hectic task as the form was 7 pages long and asked almost everything about myself and some of the particulars were unknown to me as well, hence, my dad helped me out to answer those questions. At the end of the form, there was a list of mandatory documents mentioned that were required and I started taking out documents one by one from my folder. I had all my documents in my possession, I arranged them in a particular order and was looking forward to my turn.

I was allotted the computer science branch. I wasn't interested in the same because of the complexity involved and we didn't have computer science as a subject in our school so I didn't get a chance to develop any interest or competence, but the only reason for opting for this stream was the package that followed the completion of the graduation. I wanted to secure the best possible packages offered by the likes of Google and Microsoft. In our childhood, we are told by everyone around us to follow your passion, hobby, or your dreams, but with time the majority of the population is introduced to the fact that one has to follow the path in which probability of success is simply higher. That single fact upgraded my thought about life, rather being compared with Raju Rastogi of three idiots. I could relate my life to Farhan for the first time, but the only difference between us was that he wanted to be a photographer and I didn't know what I wanted to be. I just knew that computer engineering was not my cup of tea.

"Vihaan Miglani, report to counter number three," an anonymous entity announced on the mic.

I rushed to that counter and kept my file on the table. He vetted all the documents and signed on my form while acknowledging the same and asked me to go and deposit the demand draft at the last counter with this file. It was indeed the final step towards my admission process.

"Sir, this is my file and this is the demand draft," I said to the guy sitting at the last counter.

"Son, this demand draft mentions Rs. 75,000 only," he replied.

"Yes sir," I answered.

"But it was mentioned that the demand draft should be of Rs. 1,20,000. Aren't you familiar with the notice?" he asked.

I didn't know what to say and was startled. I called my dad who was sitting towards the end of the auditorium. He started yelling at me. I requested him to calm down and come with me. He spoke to the coordinator for about 10-15 minutes or so. My dad was neither in the mood nor conscience to listen to him. He was continuously mentioning that we just have a Rs. 75,000 demand draft as it was mentioned online.

"Sir, kindly go to the head counter and inquire about it there. We can't offer your child admission without the deemed fee payment. Please arrange a new demand draft by tomorrow or I fear you might have to leave." he gave his final statement.

We visited every counter, requested a meeting with every relevant official and their respective heads, but all had the same unchanging opinion to share across with us. I had tears in my eyes because it was me who checked the fee structure and informed my dad about the same. We were finally told that the fee structure was from last year and that the same was revamped this year as declared by the government.

"Vihaan, how can you indulge in such a doltish mistake. Our resources in terms of time and money are both rendered useless. You are a grownup individual, be responsible!" my father shouted, consumed with rage.

Rage had quite a grip on me as well as the moment and hence, I replied back imprudently, "It was so difficult for you to arrange Rs. 75,000, how could you have possibly arranged almost double the amount. You have done absolutely nothing for me.".

Silence followed the thunderclap of the recent conversation. He picked up all the luggage that had accompanied us and thereafter, started walking towards the exit gate. I failed to realize how rude I was and continued following him. We took a ride through an auto to the railway station and I was able to spot tears in his eyes but my current temper was high enough to keep myself from consoling him. From Delhi to our hometown, we didn't look into each other's eyes. It was an 8-hour-long journey backed by extreme silence. I was cursing my dad and I have reasons to believe that he was also in regret but anyways, he was a villain for me at that time.

My mom was looking forward to greeting us with sweets and had also prepared my favourite food. But when she saw the expression of unshaken rage on our faces, her feelings were succeeded by obnoxious worry and she started putting forward queries, rapidly. We both refused to answer and made our way to our respective rooms. I could hear my father crying but did not bother to enter his room.

I was pondering over reappearing for the JEE mains examination next year but the thought was interrupted by the fact that my marks were indeed, not the problem and apparently, no one seemed concerned about my career or future as well. My mom procured the information of the events that followed earlier, with regards to the admission from my dad. I was absolutely certain that he would tell her anyway and hence, didn't bother otherwise.

For the next few days, neither one hosted a conversation with each other nor was ready to listen. On a particular day, I entered my dad's room to take some documents in his absence. I found a loan agreement. My body and mind were numb after reading it. The loan was against our house and he had 3.8 lakh in his account. I kept all the documents inside and rushed to the washroom. At the time, I was really ashamed since my father had submitted his house as collateral for the sake of my future. It was quite difficult for me to control my emotions, so washroom was the best place to cry secretly. I washed my face and went to the kitchen to rejuvenate myself.

I just felt like leaving home forever because my actions were adversely affecting their life. I went to my room and packed a bag. Before leaving, I intended to sincerely apologise, and therefore, I wrote a letter for my dad. Writing the letter was a much more tedious task than preparing for JEE mains itself. During the first one hour I simply wrote 'sorry dad'. That's it. But the moment I was able to figure out what should be the content for the letter, within the next 30-40 minutes, I completed a 5-page letter. I placed the same on my study table with a note aside so that they could read it after I left. I decided to leave early in the morning simply because everyone must be asleep during the early hours. Hence, I set my alarm for 4 a.m. and slept.

I woke up in the morning and looked at the watch. It was 8:30 in the morning already and instead of the alarm clock, my mom was waking me up.

"Vihaan, get up, it's 8:30 and your dad is calling you in his room," my mom said while cleaning my study table.

I forgot that I had to leave the residence this morning. I made my way to his room. He was having tea and had a letter in his hand. When I saw that letter, I realized I should not have been here.

"Dad …I... I … I".

"Sit here. I want to talk to you," my dad exclaimed.

He started laughing and suddenly his laughter became eerie. I was able to listen to the alarm clock and then I woke up and realized that it was simply a dream. I went to the kitchen to have a glass of water and without wasting another moment, I picked my bag and left. I walked for around 6-7 km in the dark. I was feeling thirsty and hungry. The best part of my planning was that it was unplanned. Neither did I have a place to stay nor the money to eat anything. I intended to go back but by then my parents must have read the letter I wrote earlier and I lacked the virtue to face them. But the hunger was unstoppable and it forced me to head back to the residence. I rang the bell hoping that my mom would run towards the door, hug me, kiss me and my dad must be crying to see me but I was welcomed with two tight slaps on each side of my face. It was a reward for the offence I committed after all. After receiving the warm welcome, I went to the room to verify the location of the letter and discovered that it was placed in its original location. It was sealed and in the exact same location where I had kept it, giving me the reason to believe that no one had got a hold of it yet. Those events confirmed the fact that taking action is of prime importance.

Like a love triangle, I was within the hate section. I believe I was neither talking to my dad or my mom, nor was the conversation being hosted from their end after what I did. When I recalled that incident, I found it funny, but it was a tense situation then. I was in guilt because both my parents were not happy with me and I wanted to apologize for my sin. I rewrote that letter and I removed that part which said that I was leaving home.

"Dad, please take this letter. Can you please read it?" I asked my dad.

"Vihaan, what is this letter about?" my dad asked.

"I intended to get something across and I was unable to speak the same so I just wrote it down. Please read it once," I said and left my home at once because I didn't want to be present there while he was reading it. I walked down the street with my hands in my pocket. After 15-20 minutes, I came back and saw my father. He had tears in his eyes and a smile on his face. He forgave me for what I did and accepted my apology.

"Vihaan, your Hindi is so bad, you must improve under any and all circumstances," my dad exclaimed and started laughing. That moment was like a sunny day after a storm. In that storm, we forgot to make any decision about my college. So, without wasting a moment, my father took me to the cybercafé to do some research and find a way.

"How can I help you, sir? Are you both trying to find something?" the owner of a cybercafé asked.

"Yes, please. We have missed the admission date of my son. Is there any way to apply now?" my dad asked.

He asked us all the details and gave us one brilliant solution. He suggested that I apply in the second round and my rank was good enough to ensure a seat. However, it was certain that I would not be able to take the branch by choice. I read everything in greater detail and explained the same to my dad. The deadline to apply was in 3 hours. We rushed home to take all the documents which were due to be uploaded. This time, the same amount was supposed to be paid online. We didn't have any card or net banking access, so the cybercafé owner did that for us and took some commission for that transaction. We managed to submit my application before the deadline. The second round was supposed to be 10 days later in college. So, till then, we had to arrange things and I, for certain, had no intention of repeating the same mistakes as earlier.

"Leaving home for college is the dream of every middle-class Indian kid—it's not just a new chapter, it's a whole new book."

Chapter 3

Wild Card Entry

"Vihaan, where is your admit card?" my mom exclaimed.

"I have already kept it with other documents," I replied to her back. Everyone was in a hurtle backed by the fact that we were leaving for Delhi. We all had a lot of pressure, and in that hustle, I forgot to perform the basic morning practice of freshening up. Father and I were ready to leave but as soon as I stepped out of the door, I got a call from my intestine. I left all my luggage there and ran towards the washroom. Meanwhile, my mom started the rant time session. She did better than Kartik Aryan from Pyar ka Punchnama. My father had a drinking problem, precisely relevant to tea drinking. Due to his haste, he had forgotten to drink tea. After so much hustle we managed to reach the bus stand on time.

I didn't sleep the whole night in excitement. So, after putting my luggage, I took a window seat to sleep comfortably, unaware of the fact that the comfort was short lived. Although I was allergic to dust, I made the extreme mistake of sitting near the window of the bus. After 30 minutes of journey, I started sneezing vigorously, my eyes were red, and I had a running nose. After 15 minutes, a guy sitting at the back of my seat started counting the number of sneezes. The journey was 16 hours long and in such a condition, it was terrifying for me. After 4 hours, the bus driver stopped the bus near a dhaba (a small roadside eatery) for lunch. Till then, the count reached 378. I had 2-3 cups of coffee and some chocolates to get some relief from that allergic cold. I didn't remember the rest of the journey because I was in a deep sleep.

"Vihaan…Vihaan, wake up. We have reached, put on your shoes," my dad whispered in my ear. I woke up instantly, it was too noisy on the bus, and I hardly saw anyone's face because of the low light. My body was too tired to walk straight, I banged my head on the pole first, then foot on the seat corner. My dad was carrying all the luggage with ease and I was carrying only 55 kg of weight out of which my body weight was 54.85 kg and the rest included some biscuit packets I bought from the bus stop. As I went down the bus, I saw a group of people sleeping in line. They seemed to be bus drivers or conductors. I was hungry but the only thing which was available there were mosquitoes. You could swallow 10 mosquitoes every 5-10 meters.

It was too late to search for a guest house and also, we didn't have any extra bucks to spend towards the same, so we decided to sleep in the waiting area of the bus stand. My dad was fully prepared for it, he took out two blankets from the bag. One blanket was so worn out that I think mom gave it to put it on the floor only. After making a proper bed out of the blankets, my dad took a rope and tied all our luggage together and the other end to his waist. I was amazed to see such life hacks. I was able to see how much responsibility a father had. He was so exhausted that he slept within a moment or two.

I woke up and found that the bus stand was empty. It seemed that there was a curfew. My dad was washing his face in the public water cooler. I moved my eyes to the place where the luggage was kept, and shouted "Dad, where is our luggage, where are my documents?"

"It's gone. You will not get admission today, so we will leave for home now," my dad replied.

Suddenly a group of people surrounded me and started staring at me,

"Vihaan, go back home."

"You must tell your dad about IIT."

"You lied to him."

That group was adamantly unanimous.

"Dad… Dad, come here," I shouted.

"Vihaan, what happened," my dad replied while waking me up.

I opened my eyes and found everything to be normal. It was 6 in the morning and most importantly the luggage was at its place.

"Nothing, dad, I just had a bad dream," I answered.

"Vihaan, you and your dreams. Now go and have a bath. There is one public bathroom, take your clothes with you and get ready. Meanwhile, I am going to that food stall for breakfast," my dad said.

I took my clothes, towel, and brush and went to the bathroom. The bathroom was not properly maintained. There were spit spots of paan on walls and dirt on the floor. The tap was broken and the valve of shower was so tight that it took 10 minutes' worth of effort to open the same. After taking a bath, I was finding difficulty in closing the earlier valve. Being an educated citizen, I should not waste water, but I failed to do so. I blamed the government for it and went outside. In India, if you fail to fulfil your moral duty, then you are liable to put blame on your government, and I did the same.

"Vihaan, you took so long, now tell me, what will you eat? I have ordered a parantha and a tea for myself," my dad said.

I asked my dad to order the same for me and opened my bag to keep my clothes back in it. While I was struggling in zipping up the bag, my dad came towards me and slapped slowly behind my head.

"Vihaan, you are putting your wet clothes with new clothes, are you mad?" my dad yelled at me.

I knew I was wrong so I smiled to lower his anger and changed the topic to my admission. I knew that he would not say anything or would not be harsh to me because it was a big day for me and I leveraged the same really well at my disposal.

After packing all our stuff, we left for college. ETA was 52 minutes, and at that time my dad checked all documents a number of times. He was tense, it was visible on his face and from his actions in a crystal-clear manner.

As soon as I entered the auditorium, there was an important announcement, "Students with a rank between 5000-25000, report to the registration desk for document verification." I rushed to desk number 5 as it was allotted to rank between 20000-25000. After waiting for 36 minutes in a queue, my turn came and a guy sitting behind that desk remembered my name.

"Hope you have everything this time," he said and took my documents. He took 2 minutes to verify it and gave one admission form which had to be submitted while branch allotment.

It was like an IPL auction, and our ranks were the same as the base price of the player. The only difference was a person with less money gets the best player. There was a huge screen in front of us which showed the number of seats left per Stream and they were calling us one by one starting from lower rank to upper. My name was announced, and I went to the desk. It was a one-minute walk but millions of thoughts were going through my mind. I was confused.

"Yes, give me your form, and tell me the branch you want," an old gentleman sitting with some files and stamps asked.

I gave my form and in a feeble voice I replied "Mechanical, Sir," I presumed him to have a hearing problem, so I said it again "Mechanical Engineering, sir."

"Okay, don't repeat it, I am not deaf," he replied and gave me a confirmation letter. I offered my apologies and left the hall.

My dad was waiting outside, he was sitting under a shed as it was raining. He was hungry but it seemed that my confirmation letter took away his hunger. I saw him happy after a long time. We went to a Dominos to celebrate. It was the very first time we were going to such an expensive restaurant.

We returned home via bus the same night. He slept despite the fact that I was feeling refreshed and energised. All I was doing was staring out of the bus window at the cityscape at night. At that time, the same environment that had given me the chills the day before, was now spectacular. People are at their worst when they do this. When everything goes our way, we are able to enjoy the ambience; otherwise, we are unable to appreciate the most valuable gift of all: life.

A couple of buses honked right in front of ours. It wasn't until I looked behind me that I realised what was making all of the noise: our bus was about to crash. A few millimetres away from where the bus was hit, I was seated. When I woke up, I was in the hospital and had no recollection of the past.

It was tough for me to open my half-closed eyes and realise what I was looking at: just hospital beds and one nurse. Eventually, I regained consciousness and discovered that a plaster had been applied to my left leg and that I had a bandage on the top of my head. It seemed as if I had hit my head and knee on the front seat of the car before getting out. Following my awakening, the physicians arrived to do a physical examination of my physical condition.

"How are you feeling right now?" the doctor asked.

"Where is my dad? I want to meet him," I asked back.

"He is fine, just tell me, is there any pain?" doctors asked again.

"Yes, doctor I am fine. Can you tell me what happened to my leg?" I inquired.

"It is just a fracture. It will be fine in a month," the doctor replied.

I started crying because my college session was starting in the next 10 days and I have a broken leg.

The doctor didn't ask any further questions and said, "Now take a rest, we will take you to your dad soon."

At 7 in the morning, one nurse came and took me to other beds with the help of a walker so that I could verify my dad, but I failed to find him.

"There is one casualty in this accident, please come with me and verify the body," the nurse said and held me tightly.

I was numb for a moment. I was in shock that I sat there for a while. 2-3 people from the hospital staff came with a wheelchair and took me to the corpse. It was the same size as my dad and I screamed so loudly that everyone got scared. They took off the cloth and I took a deep breath.

I was relieved to see that it was not my dad. It was a bad feeling, imagining your dad dead was painful.

A nurse from the corridor was coming towards me as she approached me. She asked: "Are you Vihaan Mighlani?"

"Yes, my name is Vihaan, what happened?" I inquired.

"Your dad is searching for you. He is waiting for you near your bed." She replied.

She took me to the bed and I saw my dad and I started crying. He wiped my tears and asked, "Are you fine?"

"Yes, Dad, just a small fracture," I replied. I didn't tell him about what just happened and tried to act normal. My dad just had some minor cuts and he was wearing a neckband because of a jerk in the neck. He got discharged from the hospital but the doctor asked me to stay for a day. He stayed in the waiting room that night.

We were trying to save money during the whole journey by cutting down unnecessary expenses but at last, we were indeed thrown over budget. Because of my condition, my father took the ticket of the sleeper bus and it was an extra burden on his pocket.

My father lied to my mom that we will be one day late because some paperwork is left, since my mom was eagerly waiting for me. People from the neighbourhood came to greet me. Apparently, they had planned a surprise for me but the future had plans otherwise in hold for us.

When my father and I entered our house, around 10-15 people were waiting for us already but the number seemed to be 100 considering the size of the house, which was too small. They all were in shock to see my broken leg.

"Vihaan!" My mom screamed.

By the law of nature, it was supposed to be me who would cry because of pain in my leg, but I was the one who was asking my mom to stay calm.

"Mom, it is just a fracture, nothing else. I was running on the road of my college campus and I fell down as I was not careful." My dad had asked me to tell this story.

Neighbours were enjoying the melodrama. It seemed they were in a Cinema Hall with soft drinks in their hands and enjoying the best scene of that movie. After that emotional scene got over, they congratulated me and left. They finished all the snacks that my mom arranged for them before leaving and I was sad about it.

My parents, especially my mom, treated me like a king that day because of that fracture and the fact that in a week I had to shift to the Hostel.

Next Day, my dad took me to the doctor to get my leg checked, after seeing my X-Ray report the doctor said, "The fracture is minor and you can remove it after 10-15 days. Till then you have to take complete and uninterrupted rest." The doctor was my dad's friend so he gave a spare walking stick to me and said, "Use this stick to walk, I know you have to leave for your college. Congratulations as well!"

Everyone in my family was busy packing. It seemed like I was going to be married. Shusma Aunty (our neighbour) used to come daily for an hour to gossip with my mom, but by this point in time she was already amongst the likes of our family members. She used to come at 11 in the morning and leave at 4 in the evening. She was helping my mom for the majority of time. I was enjoying her visits because I was receiving everything on my bed. Every night my dad used to give me a new lecture on life. He was trying to share his experience so that I could live alone and tackle all my problems, but I was the least interested in his lectures.

I was at the zenith of emotion, and filled with excitement as a new phase of my life was about to commence. I was already living my college days in my dreams and was planning what I would do. My luggage was ready and the tickets booked. Dad booked a train ticket this time and mom was accompanying us as well. According to IRCTC, the tickets we purchased were the cheapest available, but it seemed to be above budget to me.

We left home at 4 in the morning to the railway station. It was exactly 1 hour away from our home but we took 45 minutes to reach as roads were empty. The railway station was packed with people and it was difficult for me to walk in the crowd with a stick.

"Sir, we will take your bag. Tell us your platform number." Two coolies came and spoke

"No, no, we will manage," my dad replied.

One coolie watched my fracture so he proposed to my dad that they will pick me up and will drop me to the train and dad agreed with him. He made me sit on his shoulders and started walking towards our train. Everyone on the station was watching me and I was feeling so embarrassed. I was in guilt to see my mom and dad struggle to carry the luggage.

Coolie dropped me to our seat on the train and helped my dad to keep the luggage properly. The train was on time and we reached Delhi railway station at 5 PM in the evening. We decided to not take a hotel and left for college.

My mom was amazed when revealed to the college campus which was itself comparable to the size of a city. Last time we didn't see the hostel building as we were getting late. There was a board showing that the hostel was to the left, relative to it. Even from that point, my hostel was 700 m away. The hostel had four buildings, each designated to a particular year of students. My hostel's name was Mahatma Gandhi hostel and my room number was 126. It was on the ground floor itself. As I entered my building, I saw a food mess and a playing area on my left, and rooms towards the right. Mess was extremely tidy and big. I presumed the hostel to be in a bad condition as it was a government college but it was neat and well maintained.

I dropped a bag and went towards the playing area. There were 3 table tennis tables, 1 carrom board and at the back of that room there was a badminton court.

"Vihaan… Come here. We have a train, so let's go to your room first. You can see other things later. You have four years," my dad said.

We went to the room and it was already open. I opened the door and found there were already some people in there. I again checked the room number.

Is it room number 126?" I asked

Yes, are you Vihaan?" a boy asked.

"How do you know my name?" I inquired.

"Hi, I am Nikith, your roommate, and they are my parents," he said, and put his hand forward.

He was taller than me, around 5 feet 10 inch. His hairs were half curly and half straight. By looking at his clothes, I was able to predict that he was from a rich family. While I was observing him and his family, both parents got social and started conversing with each other. My mom even told them that I used to pee in my bed till I was in 4th Standard. While our mothers were talking about us, our fathers were busy inquiring with the security guard and hostel wards. I looked towards Nikith's face which showed a clear resemblance of embarrassment as his mom was also sharing his side of stories. After a while, Nikith's mom was helping my mom in placing my clothes and other things in the cupboard. They both took 2 hours to set it. It would have been done in an hour but my mom wanted to tell her that one of her friends is so terrible. While they were busy with their conversation, Nikith and I went out to submit our hostel form. While we were heading towards a hostel office, I was able to see a lot of parents, everyone was there with their child. Our hostel was full of parents because it was only for first year students. In front of the office, there was a long queue. We both were a little hesitant, so I initiated the conversation.

"My name is Vihaan Miglani, I am from Varanasi," I told Nikith, as I wanted to know his full name.

“I am from Chennai,” He replied.

I felt awkward asking his full name so I started talking about the JEE Mains exam and ranking. We both were not as comfortable with each other as our moms were. It took approximately 25 minutes to submit the form and we spoke for hardly 3 minutes. After submitting the hostel form, we went back to our rooms. Our parents were waiting for us so that we could all go for dinner together.

“Vihaan, wear your shoes, we are going out,” my dad told me.

“Dad, you have a train. You should leave for the station,” I replied.

My dad ignored me and asked everyone to come. I wore my new shoes which looked worse than the slippers of Nikith, and went out with everyone. We took an auto to a nearby hotel. The first thing I did as I entered the hotel was to check the price list because I knew our limitations. We had a good dinner and the food was amazing, too. For the very first time, I saw my dad wanting to pay that bill so badly that he snatched the bill from Nikith’s father’s hand and took his wallet to pay the bill. I was shocked to encounter the incident and I started wondering what if my dad is a rich guy and pretending to be a middle-class man. Maybe my dad has a bungalow and car somewhere near our house, and he owns a big business. I felt so good imagining that we are rich.

“What are you thinking, Vihaan?” my mom asked.

“Nothing…” I replied back with a smile.

"I know you must be thinking about your dream last night. Go and wash your hands. We are dropping you at your room and then we will leave," my mom said.

My mom had tears when she was leaving, but I wanted her to go as soon as possible because I was eagerly looking forward to the inception of my college life. After our parents left, I took my diary and went to the playing area which was empty and had some lights. That diary was different from others' diaries, it was a diary of my dreams, my fantasies. I used to write all those situations which happened in my mind and the ones that would have made my life better if the same were transmuted into reality. Most of the fantasies were related to some Bollywood movies like 3 Idiots, ZNMD, Rocket Singh: Salesman of the year, etc.

"Vihaan, you must come to the room and sleep. We have our orientation tomorrow at 9 in morning," Nikith shouted from the water cooler where he was filling his water bottle.

"I am coming in 5 minutes. You may sleep. Please leave the door open," I replied.

He came near me and said in a low voice "Can you come after 15 minutes? I want to do something."

"Yes of course." I instantly agreed as I wanted to spend some more time in the fresh air. The air was not that fresh scientifically as PM 10 and PM 2.5 was severely high in that area.

I was hesitating when entering the room because I knew he was masturbating so I knocked once and went towards the mess area as he didn't reply to me back. After 20 minutes he came out to throw the tissue paper in the hostel common bin. He called me back to the room and politely asked me to sleep.

I was excited for orientation but the reason for the high dopamine level in my body was my dreams. I was still in the zone where we are rich.

"Vihaan, I am not able to sleep. Are you?" Nikith asked.

"No, will you join me? I am going for a walk," I replied.

"It's already 11:30 PM and our curfew timing is 11 PM, I think. I don't want to get caught on the first day," Nikith said.

"Do you smoke?" Nikith asked.

"Smoke what?" I asked curiously.

"Cigarette, stupid!" He replied and switched on the torch in his mobile to find a switch for the room's light.

"Which mobile is it?" I inquired.

"This is an iPhone. Do you mind if I smoke in the room?" he asked.

I allowed him because I wanted to act cool in front of him. I also took one puff after he insisted that I do so. After just one puff, I was coughing badly like a TB patient.

"Nikith, does that cause throat cancer?" I asked him while coughing.

He started laughing, "Come on, Vihaan, don't act that stupid. You will not get cancer from one puff. It's your first time. You will learn to smoke easily," he threw the cigarette bud and switched off the light "Good Night, Vihaan."

It was the first time in my life that I felt this type of freedom. I took the first drag and everything was normal around me. That was the indication that college life has started and now I have to make my own decisions and have to decide for myself what was good and otherwise. I got a bit serious after the moment, since on one hand my parents were putting in a lot of effort in order to pay the fees and on the other hand, I did something that could potentially break their trust. I took my phone to see the time. My mobile watch showed 1:30 AM. I was able to hear Nikith's snoring. I stopped my mind from wandering and focused on sleeping.

"Vihaan... You must sleep now. You have to start a new chapter of your life tomorrow morning and you haven't done anything wrong, so just focus on all the good that future beholds," I told myself and slept.

"People value time differently. It's precious when someone else makes them wait, but it seems worthless when they're waiting for something they want."

Chapter 4

Let Me Complete (Present)

"Vihaan, you did a great job. Your decision to not go to IIT was best according to the circumstances. But, to be honest, I am not convinced with your story till now," he interrupted me.

"Sir, it was simply the reference for the story which I intended to share with you. Please allow me to start with the main part."

"Before you start, should we take a break? I know you have the energy to narrate your story in a go and you haven't even completed narrating from your first diary."

He left the room for a break. As soon as he left, I got up and went to see the books in his collection. Just looking at his collection, I could see the link between him and that building, because all Hindu Vedas, Bhagwat Gita, Ramayana, and books related to it were a major part of his collection. I got curious to know more about it, so without his permission I started looking into his collections and some personal stuff. I ran towards the chair and acted as if nothing had happened as soon as I heard some footsteps approaching. It was him, and luckily, I hopped onto the chair on time. If I would have gotten some more time, then I would have established his relation with that place.

"Yes Vihaan. So, in your story till now, you have reached college and a new chapter of your life is about to start. Shall we start or do you need some more rest?"

"No, sir, we may kindly start. I have already opened the diary. Here it is…"

"Pretending to be someone else is the fastest way to lose yourself completely."

Chapter 5

Swing Vote

Everyone kindly pay attention, Train No. ME1201 will depart from Gate number 7 in the next 20 minutes. I could hear that announcement as our hostel was giving me the feel of a railway station. Some volunteers, mostly second year students, were waiting for us outside our hostel like a coolie. At 9 AM, we were supposed to reach the Auditorium for orientation and seniors got the duty to take us there on time.

"Vihaan, please rush to the bathroom. Otherwise, you will be late." Nikith said while waking me up.

"Is the train on time?" I asked.

"What…? Are you still dreaming?" he asked surprisingly.

I realized that I said a weird thing. So, to cover it up I took my clothes and rushed to the common bathroom. I could see a bodybuilding competition going on in the washroom. All participants were waiting for their turn. They hardly had any muscles on their body but everyone was standing shirtless, some were showing their abs and some, their fat chest. I think they all thought physics books were enough for 17-inch biceps. I also joined the queue of bodybuilders. After me, 5 more students joined that line and I was the odd one out as I was the only one who was wearing a t-shirt. I also decided to show my 5 gm of muscles to everyone and took my t-shirt off. I got pushed from the back and was able to feel the guy who was standing just behind me. I was in the mechanical branch so this was the maximum skin contact that I could expect.

"Hi, my name is Rathik Pathak, mechanical branch, room number 124. I am from Indore, Madhya Pradesh." A guy standing in front turned and gave his full introduction.

"Hi, I am Vihaan," I replied and yelled at guys who were occupying the bathroom "Please move fast, we are getting late."

He thought I ignored him but I was stressed at that moment, because as usual, I was late.

After 15 minutes of waiting patiently, I got the opportunity to enter the bathroom and post my clothes. I realized that I didn't carry soap. I assumed that it would be there in the bathroom. I commenced real-time SWOT analysis and concluded that humans can indeed take a bath without soap as well, and hence, I just poured some water on myself and rushed my way towards my room. After getting ready, I went out to the spot where Nikith was supposed to wait for me but he was not there. There were only 8 people left, including me, so I left with them as I was not aware of the way to the auditorium from our hostel. It took approximately 6 minutes to reach the auditorium and in those 6 minutes, Rathik told me everything he could, about him. In those 6 minutes he told me about his Ex and why his mom dislikes his aunt. It was a lot of information for me to process and store even if I didn't hear what he said, in its entirety. I was trying to be on my guard when it came to making friends because I had a fact in mind that quoted, the type of friends I make is the kind of person I will become in the future. I heard this in a motivational speech on YouTube during my JEE mains preparation. My father also told me the same thing, so I was trying to figure out who is my kind or who I want to become. Till then, I had met only two people: Nikith and Rathik. They both were nice to me but it was too early to make a judgment.

The auditorium was fully packed. It had a capacity of 400-500 people but there were around 1600 students which is three times the total capacity. Students were sitting on the floor of the auditorium and some were sitting on the stairs of the stage.

"Before we start the orientation for the new batch, please stand for the National Anthem". I was about to open the door to enter the auditorium and everyone stood up following the announcement. I had only 52 seconds to figure out where I could sit and I wasted 10 seconds of them looking for empty seats. After 10 seconds I realized that if students are sitting on the floor, then all seats must be occupied. After the national anthem ended, I went to the fourth row from last as there was some space on the floor.

“Vihaan, look here” Nikith shouted.

I turned around and discovered that Nikith was calling for me “Yes, Nikith, what happened?” I asked

“I have reserved a seat for you, come fast,” Nikith replied.

From the last 10-20 minutes, I was feeling really bad as Nikith had left the hostel without me but this very gesture from him was really special. I pushed 2-3 students and reached my reserved seat successfully.

“Thanks, Nikith, for the seat,” I said.

“It’s okay. From next time, please be on time,” he replied.

During the entire search operation for the vacant seat, I had left Rathik behind and was thankful that I didn’t sit with him for the whole orientation. We all felt sleepy after 30-35 minutes, one after the other Head of Departments were coming on the podium to say a few lines for us and I was sure that they must be using the same lines from the past few decades. All HODs were 55+ so definitely there was a gap of almost 2 generations between us. While I was getting bored, Nikith took a novel out of his bag and started reading from the page where he left the bookmark. I was so disinterested in novels, that I didn’t bother to read the title of the novel either. After dozens of boring speeches, there were some cultural performances by students. The energy level of students went from -100 to +100 within a second when a group of girls came on stage for a dance performance. They started off with some Hollywood songs and ended on some Punjabi beats. Nikith was the only person who was not interested. He didn't close his novel for once, in fact, he completed his novel before the orientation ended.

"Either the orientation is too long or you are a fast reader," I said to Nikith.

"I would have taken half of the time I spent here. It is only that I was finding it difficult to read in this noise," Nikith replied.

It was almost 2 PM when we came out of orientation and we all rushed to the hostel mess as food was available from 1 PM to 3 PM only. It was my first time eating in a mess. I had missed my breakfast as I was getting late. The two bananas I ate in the morning saved me from starvation. As a child, I used to imagine college mess as the dining area of Harry Potter but it was more like a jail's mess in Hollywood movies. The food was not as good as home-made food but it was enough to fulfil my body's nutrient requirements.

Our first class was from the next day, so I went out with other students who were going to the playground as Nikith was busy reading a new novel. I left at 3:30 PM and came around 7:30 PM, almost four hours later, and my clothes were wet because of sweat.

"You should have come with us. The guy next to our room thinks he is a great batsman. He claims that he was a captain of the school cricket team, but I bowled him on the very first ball," I told Nikith while passing around his bed to reach mine.

"He must be a show off. You will find many like him here. First, tell me if you have played with water or is it sweat?" Nikith asked.

"Of course, it is sweat. Don't worry I am going for a bath," I replied.

"Good, Vihaan. Go and take a bath, then we will leave for dinner. Tomorrow, we have our first lecture, so we will sleep on time," Nikith told me.

I agreed with him because today I was late for orientation. I followed his suggestion and went to bed by 10 PM.

* * *

Our class number was FY-08, FY is not financial year. It was first year. There were around 130 students in our class and being our first class, the attendance was 100%. For the very first time in 3-4 months, I realized that I haven't achieved anything big. I thought I was in the top 1% of students in India, but that 1% was equal to the population of some European country. There were students from 3 different branches, Mechanical, Information Technology, and Civil Engineering. Purpose to mixing different branches was to help students familiarize themselves with each other better and it was practically possible in the first year as subjects were the same. This was a good initiative for mechanical students as it gave us a chance to be friends with the opposite gender because our branch had no girl. Initiative was good but execution was poor because there was a rank difference between all three branches. I was just following Nikith. Within 2 days only, he had a huge impact on me as he seemed to be a perfect man with some bad habits, but smoking is not bad as it is trending among college students. Smoking is now one of the symbols of being cool.

Nikith saw that the first bench of 5th row was empty, so he sat there. I was always a back bencher, so was hesitating a bit.

"Hi Vihaan, come, you can sit here," Rathik shouted.

As soon as I heard it, I kept my bag beside Nikith and sat with him without having a second thought. I was trying my best to avoid him, but he was everywhere. I tried not to turn back as he waved his hands as soon as I looked towards him.

The first day of class would be an introductory session between Professors and students but they didn't bother to ask our name. They directly started teaching. In fact, our chemistry professor marked the completion for the first chapter by quoting "You all must have read the chapter during JEE preparation, so it is completed from my end. Solve all the questions in the book and submit it before the next week hits the end." Before admission, they created a charade for 75% attendance by quoting it as mandatory but no teacher took attendance in the first week. Everything was moving with an extremely accelerated pace. The next thing I remembered was that the Professor was announcing the syllabus & dates for our mid semester exams. Bachelor of Technology in any major was supposed to be a marathon, but apparently was a 100-meter track race to me. When I looked around myself, everyone was sprinting and I was the only one who was sprinting and was still behind everyone.

I believe that extracurricular activities and college cultural societies were diverting my attention away from academics, therefore I chose to shift my attention to mid-semester examinations, in its entirety. But apparently, the college admin had plans otherwise for me as the gentleman announced the college elections. There was a difference of 9 days between elections and the exams. I took out a paper and ran the calculations for the time required for mid semesters preparation. In accordance with my calculations, 9 days were enough to complete the syllabus. As per my analysis, I decided to get involved in it as Nikith was standing for CR from our batch. CR is a class representative elected by batchmates.

While walking down my hostel, I was thinking about the elections and I was engrossed in such deep thoughts that I ignored 6 phone calls from my dad. My pulse rate doubled when I saw 6 missed calls. Usually, my dad doesn't call much. It is always my mom who calls daily. So, I was scared and without a second thought I called him back. With 6 missed calls, I had 6 different scenarios in my mind and all were indeed scary.

"Hello dad! What happened, is everything alright?" I enquired in a low voice.

"Yes, Vihaan we are good. Where were you? I called you multiple times," asked my dad.

"I was in the library, solving some mathematical problems," I lied in my self-defence.

"But what happened? I got scared when I saw your missed calls," I got the query further with the intention to move the conversation away from me.

"Nothing, Vihaan, I was not able to find my cheque book, so I thought you could help in finding it, but never mind, it was your mom who kept it in another cupboard and forgot to tell me." my dad replied.

"Vihaan, I came to know you have your mid semester exams. Are you studying for it?" my dad asked

"Yes dad. That's why I was in the library." I didn't want to have a conversation about exams so I told him about the elections straight away.

"Vihaan, please stay away from college elections. You should focus on your exams. We are spending on you for your studies. I hope you understand what I am trying to say." Dad scolded me and hung up the phone.

I was in regret after what my dad told me, but the same regret lasted 10 minutes. After the regret was over, I went to the mess for evening snacks and for the first time in the evening I opened my books because Nikith was in an election meeting. I wanted to be part of it but only candidates were allowed. I hardly completed the first page of the first chapter when Nikith came to the room. For the very first time, I saw him very excited.

"Nikith, what happened in the meeting? Have you also signed up for the Joint Secretary position?" I asked him in excitement.

After a 30 minutes briefing from Nikith, I understood the system of college elections. There were two parties in our college which were fighting for four positions i.e., President, Vice President, Secretary and Joint Secretary. And only 3rd & 4th year students were allowed to fight for this position. Voting for those 4 positions was like electing the Prime Minister or President of our country. Students can only vote for Class Representatives (CRs) and then CRs vote for those positions. Nikith joined NSYP (Netaji Subhash Youth Party) and for the last 5 years all four positions were from NSYP.

"I have added your name to the volunteer list, so from now on, you are also part of our party and elections." Nikith got the information across to me like it was really a big thing. For me, it was one of the biggest achievements procured from college. I was so proud of myself that I called my mother to break the news, but after 30 minutes of lecture by my mom, I hung up the phone. I don't know why both my parents were against elections. Probably because they wanted me to study all the time. For the last 3-4 years, I had been doing the same thing i.e., keeping the books open in front of me irrespective of whether I have the will to study or not, but I didn't want to do the same in college, too. Hence, I had to lie to my parents most of the time.

In college, there were only two types of students- the first ones were those who wanted to study and second were those who wanted to be the CR, or be with the CR. And the second category was a majority in the first-year batch. I was able to analyse that the majority of our seniors were either not that serious about elections or were not interested.

Keeping everything aside, we started our campaign from the very next day and drafted a well-defined plan of action. Our batch was divided into some major groups of friends and rest groups were of 2-3 students. So, we decided to target those big groups because they were the game changers. It was easy for Nikith to interact with different students but I was facing difficulties as I had the personality of that of an introvert. Daily in the evening, we used to calculate the number of confirmed votes and prepare a list of votes that were most likely to constructively convert. The same analysis made our work easier. Apart from Nikith, there were two more candidates who were participating, but our real fight was with Himanshu, as the 3rd candidate didn't have much support. Initially, we all thought that we were well educated, so these elections were different from typical Indian elections but some of the candidates were way better than our Indian politicians. Himanshu was trying to buy out the votes by bribing them in the form of a party and sharing the luxury items within his possession. He was a tall guy and always wore branded clothes. He owned a car of which I could only dream of. In fact, I couldn't even spell the name. His way of fighting elections was effective as our confirmed votes got reduced within 2 days. NSYP also approached him to be on their side because he was a capable candidate as well. As the election date was approaching our chances of winning the elections grew slim. Nikith didn't want to try any bad practices to win the elections. He wanted to fight it fair and square irrespective of the result. One night before the election, we went to the 3rd candidate and showed him our analysis and according to the same it was impossible for him to pull off a victory streak for the election, so we requested him and his supporters to vote for Nikith instead and we promised him that next year we all will support him.

Election day was a big day in college as every class was suspended and teachers were held responsible for formally conducting the elections. It took 1 hour 35 minutes to finish voting for our batch and our professor was amazed to see the strength of our batch. For the first time, 100% strength was present. The professor who was counting votes was very dramatic. He drew a table on board and started marking votes on it so that everyone could count. It was a tough competition between Himanshu and Nikith, but in the end, we lost by only 3 votes. We were shocked to see that the 3rd candidate did not receive a single vote, which further transmutes into that fact that he didn't even vote for himself. We went to him because we thought he supported us, but Himanshu pulled off cunning politics towards the end. We thought that the 3rd candidate was a genuine candidate but he was a dummy candidate instead and was placed with the simple intention to confuse us. The list we prepared was 99% correct as all voted for us from whom we were expecting. In fact, we had more votes, but we lost because of that 3rd candidate. I was outrageous at the moment and proceeded towards him with the intention to propose a challenge for a real fight, but Nikith stopped me and asked me to come with him. I don't know how Nikith was keeping his temperament so cool.

After the declaration of results, we straight away went to the candidate who was standing for the Presidential position with the intention to warn him. When we told him everything, he replied by telling us that we are new to it and it happens every year. You should now both focus on my win as the President.

We promised him to show our support and went to our room for lunch.

“Nikith, don’t worry, we will support them now and will win the presidential election” I told Nikith.

“Vihaan, don’t get carried away with it so easily. It is all politics. Now, we are of no use to them as we have lost” Nikith said and went to the room with his lunch.

I thought Nikith was sad because of his defeat, and that’s why he was talking like this. I decided to support NSYP because I was volunteering for them and thus felt that it was my duty.

During and throughout the elections, Nikith was managing his studies well. On the other hand, I hadn’t opened the first page of any book. In fact, I missed some lectures because of an election meeting. Nikith slept after that, and without wasting time, I went to the meeting room for our Party because we had only 15-16 hours to convert as many votes as we could. They all were discussing the votes and my work was to write down the names as they said. I now realize that I was never important to them but at that time I was in a separate zone. My urge to help them was so high that I stayed the whole night with them, even skipped my dinner. I came back to my room at 5:30 in the morning to take 2-3 hours of sleep before elections started.

Nikith didn’t bother to waste his time on the election. He went to the library, and I was standing outside the Auditorium where all CRs were going one by one to cast their votes. UG head declared the result early as it was a one-sided victory for our party, NSYP. All four positions were again secured by us. As soon as they declared the result, all party members and supporters went beyond control. It seemed like a full-blown festival. Everyone was enjoying the true meaning of ecstasy and were dancing in sweet joy. We all marched towards the college gate in cars. It was one kind of a victory rally. I called Nikith to break the news but he didn't pick my phone so I texted him and went to the lounge with everyone for the victory party.

My adrenaline level was at its peak because I was experiencing such a moment of accomplishment for the first time in my life and it was the first time I was going to a lounge as well. I adjusted myself in someone's car, whom I had met for the first time only. He turned on his speakers in volume and played some Punjabi songs. Speed of the car was accelerating in accordance with the beats. I was barely able to move my hands and head as 8 people were sitting in a 5- seater car. I was sensing immediate danger but I kept telling myself that everything is normal and perfect. When we reached the lounge the very first thing that came to my mind was "I should have avoided it". I sat in one corner with some food and was waiting for everyone to finish and get back to the hostel with them. After 30 minutes into the longue I could only smell alcohol and Chicken. Everyone was so busy dancing and drinking that they forgot about time. The party ended when longue owner told us to leave and gave us the bill. Bill was 1.65 Lakhs, and all four candidates were shocked to see the bill. They all went out for a meeting and after a few minutes they called some volunteers including me.

"Guys, we have a problem. Our budget was 70,000/- but the bill is 1.65 lakh, so I will ask everyone to contribute. There are around 200 students so if they can pay 500 each then we can pay our bill." the President addressed us.

We followed him and stood beside him as he was making an announcement. Within seconds, most of the students ran from there because they didn't want to contribute. At last, only 50-60 people were left who were ready to contribute and they managed to give the amount, but they were 8000 short. That day itself I had received Rs. 10,000/ from home as a 3-month expense. I didn't want to use that money, but I don't know why I trusted the president as he promised me to return the money in the next 2 days. I gave 8000 rupees. The moment I handed my money to them I realised that I had made a mistake. Whole night I was in someone's flat nearby college because we missed the deadline of entering the college. Our college gates opened at 6 in the morning and that day I was the first to enter the college. College was empty like a ghost place and the sports complex and parks were full of faculty members and their families. I was shocked to see so many faculty members at one place. I thought they only used to gather at some college events only. I was so sleepy at that time, but even then, my mind started planning a mass murder event of my professors. As exams were approaching, it was the only way to tackle it. I was heading towards my room while refurbishing the plan in my mind. I was just about to execute the plan in my mind when I realised that I had left my wallet in the flat. I ran around 3.5 km back to the flat with a constant speed of 15-20 km/hrs. It was my best running data till date. I entered my room around 7 in the morning and without disturbing Nikith I laid down on my bed for a power nap before morning class.

"Vihaan, so how was your party last night? I heard that your bill was in lakhs. Is it true or just a rumour?" Nikith asked me while waking me up for class.

I woke up instantly as I realised that I have to take money from the president. "Yes Nikith, it is true," I replied back.

"I hope you were not involved in any trouble last night," Nikith said and picked his clothes and went to take a bath. I didn't tell him that I also contributed some amount last night because I was sure that I would get my money back. After waiting for 2 days, I went to the president's room for money.

"Hi sir, I want those 8000 rupees that I gave that night," I asked him straight away.

"Welcome Vihaan, please have a seat. Apologies for the messed-up condition of the room," He replied

"No, Sir, I am fine. I am getting late for my class. Can you please give me my money?" I asked again.

"Vihaan, you know that mid semesters are coming, so focus on your exams, now. There will be some delay in the payment as I am not able to go to admin, so you can come after the last exam. If you need any help apart from it, you have my number." He gave me an assurance along with some past first year question papers for practice.

My mind was so confused at that time because on one hand I was not prepared for exams and on the other hand there was this huge financial burden. If I would have invested that money in stock, I would have gained something, but right now, I wanted my principal amount back. I had no choice other than to wait for some days and focus on exams. I had 2000 bucks, so it was enough for a month at least. Somehow, I managed to give my exams properly. Properly means that I was getting passing marks in all subjects. After my last exam, I called him but he was not answering and his room was also locked from outside. Next day, the same thing happened and I panicked. Nikith was able to notice a change in my behaviour after that party. So, after dinner, Nikith came near my bed and asked "Is there something wrong? After that election party, you are behaving differently. Tell me everything that happened that night." Without having a second thought, I told him everything and I was able to see anger on his face. He literally abused me for lending my money to some unknown person.

"Vihaan, are you a fool? How can you give a huge amount without even knowing him?" Nikith shouted.

"But he is the President of our college, so everyone knows him, and this was an official party from college, that's what he told me," I replied in a lower voice.

"You are a complete idiot. But it is not your mistake, because you are from a small town, you haven't seen the outside world. Don't worry now, we both will go to the college admin to complain about him, because he will not give your money back for sure," Nikith said and went to his bed.

I knew I had screwed it up but was happy with the gesture shown by Nikith towards my problem. We both went to the admin to complain against the president. After spending hours in admin's office, I got only 6000 rupees. It was a mutual agreement, and I was happy that I was able to recover the majority of my money and it was Nikith who helped me since otherwise he wouldn't have paid me anything. It was my first investment and I exited at a loss of 25% on principal so you can clearly call it a bad trade but there was an emotional gain. This incident helped me realize whom I could trust.

"Vihaan, 2000 bucks is a huge amount for your father, so call him and tell everything that has happened to you in the last 20 days," Nikith ordered.

I fulfilled his command and called my dad to narrate the story, but the story I told him was totally different from what had actually happened. I just told him that I had joined some robotics society so there was an entry fee of 2000 rupees. So, after that I was in a safe zone because I knew my father would not scold me for spending money on such an activity. This kind of behaviour made Nikith upset because I lied to my father who was working extra for my fees and expenditure. But that day, I realised I am not a kid anymore, and things have changed, my dad and mom had expectations from me. They were ready to spend money on my studies ignoring the fact whether their pocket allowed it or not.

"Subha jaldi uth jata hu
Par ab koi bus wala intezaar nhi krta
Roz alag kapde pehen nikal jata hu
Ab roz ek jaise kapde nahi pehenne padte
Dekho main bada ho gaya

Papa ke godh bhi utni hai aur maa ka aanchal bhi
Par ab main usmay sama nahi pata
Dekho main bada ho gaya

Badal ab bhi garajte hai
Barsaat ab bhi vaise hi hoti hai
Bas ab koi kashti nahi tairthi
Na koi keechad se khelta
Dekho main bada ho gaya

Jaadugar se ab nafarat se ho gyi hai
Aur pariyo ke duniya ke darwajay band
Dekho main bada ho gaya

Neend raat ko ab bhi aati hai
Par lori nahi sunata koi
Dekho main bada ho gaya

Mummy papa ke ungli thamay chala tha
Ab unhone meri thaami hui hai
Dekho main bada ho gaya

Bachpan mein jo chahta tha wo aaj ho gaya
Dekho main bada ho gaya"

"First love hits hard, but if it turns into a rejection, it can haunt you forever, making you feel like a lifelong loser."

Chapter 6

The Third Wheel

After securing a position in the bottom 10 of my batch, and Nikith in the top 10 of my batch, we moved to the second semester with similar goals. He wanted to secure the 1st Position and I wanted to be in the top 10 at least. I promised myself to study daily, but the motivation lasted only for about 3-4 days since this was the most happening time of the year in terms of our college. In 320 pages of our college brochure, only 8 pages were useful for students and those pages were of college festivals or campus placements. Hence, we were concerned only about two things. As of now, it was the Festival Season for us and placement season for the 4th Year students. Placement season began from 1st January to 31st January and festival season from 1st February to 15th February every year. But preparation for the fest began from 1st January itself because our college claimed to organize the biggest cultural fest of Delhi, so, for such fest, we are looking at a huge investment in terms of both time and money.

Companies were recruiting 4th year students and the fest committee was recruiting volunteers from the first year. Companies were offering money for slavery and Committee was offering a position to furnish it to the companies for slavery. Around 400 students from the first year registered to volunteer. This time, it was the opposite. Nikith registered himself to volunteer and I decided to stay away from all these activities because my past experience was not the best. The class strength was reduced to 40%, because everyone was busy in meetings or some work related to Fests. Nikith was also busy most of the time, and hence, I was alone in class and my room. I had no other choice than to talk to Rathik. With time, I realised that Rathik was not as I had imagined. He was someone you could hang around with or probably he was the only one I could have spent time with, and that's why I was enjoying his company. But somehow, we became good friends and started sharing things with each other. After spending some time with him, I got to know a lot about Rathik's nature. He was the one who loved to share his incidents or stories with everyone as he was an extrovert personality, backed by the very same fact, he could chill with anyone. He was totally opposite of Nikith. But with such nature, he still struggled to make good friends. I believe the reason was that he had a great sense of emotional balance and was always looking for ways to get the most out of every situation. His stories were the best part of him; they were like something out of a Bollywood movie script; they were hard to believe, but every one of them was 100 percent true for me, and I was quite startled. I was going to be a part of his story for the first time in the future since he included me in one of the most essential aspects of his life.

One day, I was busy copying an assignment when he approached me.

"Vihaan, I think I am in love with some girl," Rathik told me while blushing.

"Who is she? Is she from our batch?" I asked curiously.

"No, she is from the FY-02 batch, IT branch. Her name is Rashi… Rashi Mittal," he replied.

"Let's go to their class. I want to see that girl." I took him outside their classroom. I wanted to see who she was for myself. When I saw her, I realized why Rathik liked her. She was someone with whom you can fall in love with at first sight. She was pretty, with long hair and dimples on both sides of her cheeks. Her complexion was a little dark in colour and her dressing was simple. I resisted myself not to like her. Since Rathik had a crush on her, I was strictly maintaining the bro code.

It was the first time I saw her, and after that, I used to see her frequently. I also had a crush on her after the first one-sided meeting, but I was not interested in any relationship because I wasn't confident about my looks and personality. While everyone was enjoying the festive season, and stayed for the same, I had to head back to my residence for my cousin's wedding. For the first time after my admission, I was going home. During winter break, I had stayed in Hostel. I was not excited since I wanted to stay in the college, but I had no choice. It was supposed to be a 7-day trip but I came back to the college in 4 days. And when I came back, everything had changed. The canteen area was occupied by cultural societies for the PR Desk and the sponsoring brands were conducting some fun activities. I noticed that the interaction between boys and girls had increased. Before that, groups were divided on the basis of gender, but slowly, they were getting mixed. I called Nikith, but he was busy with the fest's work so I went to the canteen in search of my batchmates. There, I saw Rathik was sitting with Rashi, and I was shocked to see that, because within four days, they had become friends. For the first time I was feeling jealous and angry, while also being unable to control my emotions. Rathik called me to the table and offered me a seat.

"Rashi, he is Vihaan. Vihaan Mighlani." Rathik introduced me.

"Hi…" I waved my hand.

"Hi Vihaan, I am Rashi from the IT branch." She introduced herself and brought her hand forward to shake hands. Her hands were too soft. I think for the first time in my life I touched some girl and my testosterone level was raised.

She was there in front of my eyes for approximately 40 minutes, and out of those 40 minutes, my eyes were looking at her for around 30-35 minutes.

"Rathik, when did this happen? Are you guys dating?" I asked him as soon as she left for her lecture.

"No, Vihaan, we are not dating. She was working on some project and she required a mechanical guy for it, so I joined. I don't think she likes me now, but I am trying," he replied.

"Oh, okay!" I replied. I was relieved when I heard that.

"She is mine, so you can find someone else," he said and started laughing. I joined him.

Within 2-3 days, I got frank with her, and also started following her on social media. I stalked her within 10-15 minutes after she accepted my request. After seeing 70+ posts and reading all her captions and comments, I figured out that she was single. One day, all three of us were sitting in the Open Amphitheatre. It was a picnic spot for all students in winters because of the unparalleled sunlight. Rathik went to the canteen to buy some snacks. Meanwhile, Rashi looked towards me and asked, "Am I beautiful?" I started stuttering "Why are you asking?"

"I know you stalked me on social media that day", she said.

"Which day?" I asked, sounding confused.

"Don't lie, you liked my 2-year-old post," she replied.

I was speechless after that. "Vihaan, you can say if you want to say something. We are friends now," she replied.

I picked my bag and said "Rashi, I have some work, so I may have to leave. Bye!"

She started laughing with her hand on her face "Vihaan, you are too cute. Bye."

At that moment, I went mad. A girl saying cute to me was like a 1 in a billion chance, and that too became a reality on that very day. I rushed towards the concert ground as Nikith was working there and I was unable to control my excitement. I told him everything.

“Vihaan, my boy, you are in love,” Nikith said in excitement.

“I think so, but Rathik was the one who liked her. What should I do?” I asked

“You don’t have to do anything. Just control your emotions because love is something that can break your heart. If she likes you, then she will give you the hint automatically.” He gave me a good piece of advice.

As the Fest was approaching, the vibe of the college was funnelling into a grand celebration. The classes were officially suspended for a week due to the fest. All first-year students were way too excited, because after 2 years of struggle in JEE coaching, it was a reward. Three days before the fest, the pre-fest event started. The area near the canteen was full of students, in a blink you could see 500+ students at once. It was that crowded. While everyone was busy taking part in activities or spectating, participants Rathik and Rashi were missing. I called them around 5 times each, but no one was picking up my phone. I was feeling irritated and jealous at that time. I went to the classroom as I was feeling breathless in the crowd. My heart was broken when I saw Rashi and Rathik sitting in the classroom. I acted like I was okay to find them there.

“Hi Vihaan,” Rashi said, waving her hand towards me.

I waved back and replied “Hi. What are you doing here?”

“Nothing, we were just discussing about the project we are working on,” Rathik replied.

I knew that Rathik was lying to me and something was there between them. I just got carried away with things Rashi said to me on OAT and the gain in my confidence was wiped off on that very day. After that, I was feeling uncomfortable around both of them so I went to Nikith, so that I could divert my mind, but Nikith touched the live wire with his wet hands.

"So, you are not comfortable with the bonding between Hrithik and Rashi, right?" Nikith asked me to confirm my feelings with my expression on my face.

"I know I can't lie to you because you already know the truth, so let it be. I don't have time for these things, I am here to study, and my pocket doesn't allow me to afford a girlfriend." I replied with tears in my eyes.

Nikith started laughing "Vihaan, we have a small party tonight in our room, so be ready for that and chill."

I knew the party meant alcohol, chips and cigarettes, and out of the three, I was the chips guy, so I was not excited for the same. I just sat with them for a while and after they were a few pegs down I left the room with my diary and went to my favourite place near the badminton court. I hardly go there and sit but when I am upset that place helps me to bring out my emotions and funnel the same into my diary. Every time I went there, Nikith never came and disturbed me or poked me because he wanted to give me space. That day, I was full of emotions. For the first time I was not able to write anything. I wanted to call my mom and share everything with her because she understands me really well but it was too late to call at that time. Our hostel security guard was so caring that at times he used to pack food for us so that we could have it after the class. He saw me sitting alone there and banged his wooden stick on the ground to grab my attention.

"Hi, every week at least once I see you sitting here at night and writing something. But today you haven't opened your diary and you are just looking at the sky." The guard said in a soft voice.

"I am just looking for hope in the sky," I replied.

He laughed and said "Pollution level is poor in Delhi, so I don't think there is any hope for the same." He paused for a while and said "I know it is difficult to survive alone in this college, every year I see one or two students committing suicide. Not only are the students depressed, we are also the same sometimes. I haven't seen my wife and son for the last 6 months. Like you, I also have my diary with whom I share everything. That diary knows more about me than my wife."

He kept his stick aside and sat with me. He sat around 15 minutes with me and was helping me to find hope in the sky but as he already told us, we were only able to see black sky. He helped me realise that everyone in this college has friends but is still alone. No one feels the loneliness in day time and one can feel it only when sleep betrays at night.

I was sad because of Rathik and Rashi, but that dug up all my insecurities and failures in my life. They both acted as a catalyst to increase the sadness as a by-product in my life. Next morning, all the emotions were gone. Like everyone else, I was also excited for the fest. I was able to see that Rathik and Rashi were getting close to each other, but I controlled my emotions, and instead of getting jealous I accepted it and tried to enjoy it with them. Nikith's work for the fest was finished, so he also joined us, and he made it easy for me to control my emotions.

The day for which we had waited for a month was here; the first day of the cultural fest. College was overcrowded and there were a lot of DU students. For the first time, I was able to see that the ratio of girls to boys was 1:1, but it was temporary. Enjoying the fest alone is boring so I joined the group of Rathik, Rashi, and Rashi's friends. Nikith was also part of our group but he was a special guest as he was busy with Fest work. First two days of the fest were really good and I was able to overcome my obsession for Rashi and by the end of the second day, I was perfectly fine and moved on properly. Third day was the best day of the fest as there was DJ night as the last event of the cultural fest. Excitement levels of all students were at lifetime high. The excitement was reflected from everyone's clothes, as all were well-dressed, reflecting majority of the colours on the spectrum, the bright ones to be precise. Atmosphere was full of energy and the ambience, beautiful. The DJ night was supposed to start at 7 PM. Everyone in our group wanted to have some hard drinks so we all went out for the same. It was difficult for me to believe that they all were fond of drinking. Again, I was just a spectator. I never find myself comfortable when someone around me gets drunk, but at that time I had no other choice but to be with them. They finished one whole bottle and mixed one bottle in a Pepsi pet bottle so that they could drink while attending DJ night. After getting drunk, Rashi was not able to walk properly, and as I was the only sober one, hence, it was my duty to handle them. We walked towards the sports ground where DJ night was happening and I was holding Rashi's and Rathik's hand. My mind was again at the same spot, I didn't want to leave Rashi's hand but I did it purposely because I didn't want to hurt myself.

According to my analysis, there were around 25000 people attending DJ night and out of those, 20000 people were either drunk or high. There was a layer of smoke all over the ground. That smoke was either from joints or cigarettes. I didn't find the place appropriate enough to enjoy as people were having drunk fights and some boys were beating students just for fun. All barricades were broken and the total number of students was more than the ground's capacity. I don't think anyone was bothered about anything; they were all dancing on every song that was being played. They were performing bhangra dance forms on romantic songs as well. I was not able to enjoy it properly as Nikith was with his team, and was feeling a little bad seeing Rashi and Rathik dancing together. I decided to go back to my room, so I told Rathik that I am leaving. I don't think he even listened to what I said. I took a long cut as that path was empty.

"Vihaan, please stop, where are you going?" Rashi shouted while chasing me.

"I am going to my room. I am not feeling well so I will go and sleep," I replied and stopped for her.

She came towards me and held my hand and said "Come with me, you are not going anywhere," she tried to drag me but I resisted. I looked straight in her eyes and we both were standing quietly just looking towards each other. Slowly, she put her hand on my heart and instantly my heartbeat jumped to 150+. It was so quiet out there that I was able to hear my heart pumping. I dragged her hand from my chest and asked her to go and started walking towards the hostel. She pulled me towards her and held my face with both her hands and kissed. Unintentionally, my hands moved towards her face and kissed her back as well. She moved her hair to one side and lowered the strap of her dress. I started biting on her neck and instantly I stopped. She was not in senses at that time and I just ran away from there. Without looking back and having a second thought, I ran with maximum speed and stopped only after I reached my room. After 20 minutes, I took my phone and typed a long message to Rashi but I was not sure whether I should send it or not, so I deleted it and tried to sleep. I was awake when Nikith came but I pretended I was asleep. I got scared when I saw Rashi in my room.

"Vihaan.... Vihaan...... Vihaan" Rathik tapped on my shoulder as I was lost in my dreams and I took a deep breath. It was like someone took me out from a trap and my vision was blurred for a moment. To my surprise, I had never gone to the hostel and nothing had happened between me and Rashi. I was still in the concert ground. It was all my imagination. This happened during JEE mains as well. I was thankful that nothing had happened in real life. I was forcing myself to dance and not think about my dream, to be more precise, my imagination. I was not able to look towards Rashi as it reminded me of my imagination and I was a little uncomfortable with her.

That event ended peacefully and I managed to pretend that everything went along fine. I just kept my distance from her after that and she was able to notice that I was avoiding her, but it was fine for me. After everything was wrapped up, Nikith and Rathik got together and went to our room. Rathik stayed with us that night because he was drunk and we couldn't have taken the risk of leaving him alone. Rathik slept within seconds only and I confirmed it after slapping him 2-3 times and he didn't respond. After this confirmation, I told everything that I imagined during DJ night to Nikith. After narrating everything, he just replied "okay… good night." It took me around 30-35 minutes to tell everything and he just said anything related to it. After that, every 2 minutes, Nikith was saying the same thing again and again. Then I realised he was high so I locked the door as there were two people in our room who were not in their senses, and I slept.

Everyone had different memories from last night, for the next 3 days everyone was busy either narrating their story or listening to someone else's. They all had some witness as a proof of the memory but I had different memories from others. Which doesn't exist in reality, but for me, it was more than real. In my mind, that memory was true and it was sending a signal in accordance with the same. The worst part of all was the reputation of Rashi in my head. She was really a nice girl and a good friend. Like I started ignoring Rashi and her image in my mind got changed. At the same time, I wanted it to happen in reality because somewhere I had feelings for her. My diary was the only one who knew about it as it understands me and my feelings.

“Moving on is hard, but it’s harder when the world expects us to keep living after losing our hope with the ones we loved.”

Chapter 7

Malignancy

Our second semester ended in the blink of an eye and the only implications were the participation in the fest and especially the DJ night. On the day of the last exam, I realised that I had messed up this semester as well and the promise I made to myself at the inception of the semester had gone in vain. I had a fear of getting some backlogs this semester and Nikith was hoping to be the topper again. In one year, Nikith became an idol for me, for he was perfect in every field. Like others, he also had a bad habit of drinking, smoking and many more but he had a balance in his life and I tried to learn it but its implementation seemed impossible for me.

After our exams got over, everyone started packing their bags as we had to vacate the hostel. 80% of students were going on some vacation with their friends, including Nikith and Rathik. Even Rashi was going with them. Due to financial problems, I headed back home. With all my luggage, I went to the bus stop and took a bus from there to my home. Apparently, I was getting lonely after all. After that fest, the time spent with my friends got reduced to half and I had a fear of losing everyone as they all were going on a trip and I would not be a part of their memory. Everything was a part of my imagination at this point, I was living in a real world with experiences derived from an imaginary one.

I was going to my hometown after the completion of a year. I met my parents once at some relative's function, but it was a huge transition for me as life in Delhi is totally different from life in Varanasi. My dad was waiting for me at Bus stop. I was expecting my mom to be with him but she was waiting for me at the residence. We took a rickshaw to the home and during the whole journey my dad was asking me questions about my college life and friends. He was sounding excited and at the same time my mind was on the trip only. I was imagining what I would be doing if I was with them. As expected, my mom was waiting for me at the door with a Pooja thali in her hands. All these gestures were increasing the level of my guilt. They didn't ask my numbers or position in class because they assumed that I am a bright student and I must be doing well.

"Mom, you have lost so much weight within a few months. Are you not eating well or is it due to stress?" I asked my mom after she finished her prayer.

"Vihaan, I am good. I think I am losing some stored fat which is good for me I think," she replied.

I felt something was not correct but I ignored it for a while as I was already sad. I left my luggage out and went to my room to check. It was as I had left it, but much cleaner. I slept for 3-4 hours as I was tired. I was not in the mood to wake up but I heard my mom was puking. I rushed towards her, but my dad stopped me. He asked me to sit.

"Dad, what is happening? I know something is wrong and serious. Please tell me," I asked.

Till the time my dad could frame something and reply back, my mom came out and said "Vihaan, I think you have a right to know what is going on. Before I explain everything, go get me a glass of warm water".

I ran to the kitchen and got her what she demanded and sat with her. "Mom, please tell me everything, I hope you will not lie."

"Vihaan, last month, when I vomited, there was some blood, so we went to the doctor for a check-up. After some tests, I was diagnosed with Breast Cancer, Stage 4. Doctors are saying that it is curable but we can't afford the full treatment, so doctors have given me some medicine so that I can live more than expected."

When I heard it, my heart missed a beat and my body was dead beat numb. I was not able to feel the ground under my feet for the entire duration of the conversation. My mom held my hand tightly. I hugged her and burst into tears and at that moment I didn't want to leave her, so I hugged her even tightly. My mom was also crying at that moment, but my dad was wiping our tears with a dealer's face. He was controlling his emotions as he wanted to be a strong father and husband.

"How much time do you have?" I asked my mom.

"According to doctors, I may survive 2 months, and if the medicine works, then 3 months," she replied.

"Dad, why are we not taking her to a good hospital? We have to save her, dad," I told my dad in a loud voice.

"Vihaan, calm down. We both have already discussed this. Even if we will sell everything, we can afford 50-60% treatment and we have to give your college fees also." My dad replied.

I don't know why he was sounding so practical at that time. It was impossible for any human being to react practically in this situation, especially for me. We all had a long discussion over it and we reached the point of no discussion as we all were not on the same table and it was my mom's life, so she was the one who needed to take a final call. After the useless discussion, I went to my room and opened my diary. I wanted to write everything that was going inside my head but tears were spilling the ink and my feelings were getting blurred. It was the first time in my life I wanted to die as I was not able to handle the pain and burden of losing my mother and the burden of my mom sacrificing her life for my studies. I wanted to quit, but quitting was not an option then. I was preparing myself for the loss I was going to bear, and at the same time, I decided to stay with my mom and make her happy for all the time she had with us. My dad took command for all household work and planned some events for her.

In our house, we all had a smile on our face but from inside everyone was dying a bit, daily. We all cried when we used to be alone. I have seen my dad and mom crying a lot of times secretly. When I came from college, I was thinking of working on my skills, as I was way behind everyone in college, but instead of enhancing practical skills, my emotional skills were getting sharpened. I just ended contact with the rest of the world, which means Nikith, Rathik and Rashi. They used to call me and even text me but I didn't reply back. My fear of losing people became stronger as I was about to lose one of the most important people of my life. Daily, I had suicidal thoughts in my mind and I wanted to discuss it with my dad or Nikith, but I didn't. As the days were passing, my fear was increasing and I was marking the number of days left on the calendar behind my diary.

My mother and I had a very different bond than my father, and it was completely understandable why my mother's love was stronger than any father's. She is the one who looks after you before you arrive on the planet. Instead of expressing my affection for her, I used to scream at her for all of her mistakes. I began to see that the things for which I chastised or yelled at her were not her faults, but rather her love.

One morning, I woke up and I came to know that my mom lied to me. She was lying on her bed and her diaphragm was in resting position, her hands were blue and face was pale. I went close to her and touched her forehead. Her body was cold as ice. She said that she would survive at least 2 months, but left us 25 days before doctors predicted.

My dad asked me to be with her and went out to call the neighbours. He came back after 5 minutes with 3 of our neighbours and asked me to move aside. Her saree was wet from my tears from the place where I kept my head.

Four of them, including my dad, picked my mom and kept her on the floor in the centre of the living room. It was the first time I saw a dead body, and that too, of my mother. I don't know from where my dad was getting the power to lift her without giving support on her lower back. It must be hurting her, but her soul was free from the body to feel any kind of physical pain. My mind was not ready to digest the death of my mother and when she was lying on the floor covered with white cloth, my mind was hoping that she would wake up and say that she is fine. The cotton in her nose must be causing suffocation and her ears were also closed so that she can't hear me crying. Being the only child, it was my responsibility to perform the last rites. I wanted to delay the rituals, so that I could see my mom for more time, but within 2 hours of death, we took her to the cremation ground. The body decomposes quickly so we had to perform every ritual on time. According to our culture, a bride leaves home for cremation in her marriage dress. Our relatives and some of our neighbours dressed her properly and did some makeup. She was looking pretty in the lehenga. There were many things going around me but my mind was just busy accepting the truth. It was the first time I was entering a cremation ground and I was able to feel the pain of other people there. It is really tough for a person to burn their loved ones. All rituals performed had some meaning but the irony was that Pandit put around 2 kgs of ghee in one go on her mouth. When they asked me to light her up, I burst into tears and got down on my knees. My father helped me to perform the last ritual. I was just hoping that she would wake up from there. As a matter of fact, 80% of the wood was already burnt. The ray of hope was still there.

When I came back from the cremation ground, I saw a missed call from Nikith. For the first time, I called him back. I didn't have enough power to speak on the phone and I just could hear his voice asking me if everything was fine or not. I hung up the call and texted him and told him about my mom. He tried to give me condolences but only the person who was suffering could have understood the pain.

The house was not home anymore. It was like a ghost house where two hopeless males lived. But soon, we realised that we have to resume our life from where we left, so we started performing our daily work after the 17th day of death. Things were getting normal day by day but I was getting hallucinations of my mom. Our daily activities got normal but the state of our mind was still the same. I was stressed with the fact that she sacrificed her number of days for me. My second semester result acted as salt on my wounds. I got supplementary in two subjects. I wanted some guidance at that time because from one year I was lost, and after my mom, I was broken. And dad was not the right person to ask from, as he was already sailing in the same boat. So, I called Nikith and talked to him. I really felt good after talking to him. He was somewhere angry with me as I didn't share anything with him. According to him, I broke the law of friendship as friends share both happiness and sorrow with each other. We talked for around 1.5 hours and it was the first time, including college, that we talked for 90 minutes straight. When I was about to hang up the phone, he asked, "Vihaan… I know you must have thought about committing suicide and this thought must have crossed your mind multiple times. Am I correct?"

"I…. I…" I stammered for a while and then admitted the truth.

"This is life, and people suffer far more than you are suffering. Suicide is not an option or a solution here. You have to fight back," he replied.

I interrupted him and said "Nikith, I know that, but it is always easy to be on the other side of the problem, giving advice or motivating people. I really don't know what is correct at this time. No one wants to die at any point of his/her life, and I don't have control on my thoughts right now, so you better not give me advice without feeling my pain."

"I know Vihaan, I can't feel your pain, but yes, I am in a good state of mind so I can think practically and as a good friend I am advising you the best. Dying is an easy option any day for you, but you will create problems for others, especially your dad. And I don't want to lose you, buddy. Keep one thing in mind, if anytime you are having such thoughts, you can call me and if you do anything stupid you will not hurt yourself but your stupidity can kill your dad." He replied. Just then, due to insufficient balance in my phone, the call got dropped.

His last line opened my eyes and gave me a reason to live or survive. For my dad, too, I was the only reason to live and work hard, as I was the only person left on this planet for him.

*"They say when life gives you lemons,
make lemonade. But what if they're rotten?
You're left with bitter lemonade, and sometimes,
that's all life serves you."*

Chapter 8

The Open Mic

College vacations were coming to an end. It was time to pack the bags and leave for Delhi. There was a time when I didn't want to go back home, and now, I didn't want to leave it. My 6 months plan for college life was ready on paper and it was a Do or Die situation for me. I wanted to do it for my mom and dad. So, without wasting any time, on the first day, I got all my books from the library and started preparing for the supplementary. The aim of my life was clear at that point. My focus was only on studies and placements. For the initial 10 days, I worked really hard and followed my daily schedule properly. It was like working out in a gym with a pre-workout. But as time passed, the impact of that pre-workout was getting low and I started skipping my routine work. My efficiency got low and it was directly affecting my mental health. My social interaction was approaching zero at that time and I was getting regular panic attacks. I was not aware of what panic attacks were, but yes, all these symptoms prove that they were the same. Nikith and

Rathik were trying their best to lighten up my mood but I started ignoring them, too. I was in that state of mind where I didn't want to connect emotionally with anyone as I knew, at some point of time they would leave me alone. If a woman who gave you birth can leave, then your friends can, too.

I was broke from all sides - financially and emotionally. I knew I couldn't fix the emotions but I could work to ease the financial burden on my dad. I joined a call centre and took a night shift there. The call centre was near my college, so it was easy for me to travel. It was kind of telesales and they were offering me 6000 per month, which was a huge amount for me, so without looking into the company's profile and job description, I accepted their offer. After joining the call centre, my schedule got so tight that I hardly got time to complete my sleep. I was sleeping around 3-4 hours on average. After a few days, I found something fishy as we were getting orders of books at night, and at each alternate day, some police constables used to come and collect some cash from the owner. I told this to Nikith and he was also doubtful about the company so he decided to order a product from that company. With one call he realised that the company was selling alcohol in black, along with hash and weed. After I got to know the reality, I should have left the company, but I didn't. Nikith was forcing me to leave as it was a risky and dangerous job, but I refused his suggestions and requests because I wanted to earn money. I worked for around 25-27 days and I was about to get my first salary but the Narcotics Department of Police seized all their products and arrested all their employers including me, during the raid.

Finally, I was in jail, too. I was arrested for a crime which I never committed. They took us to the police station and gave one chance to call anyone for bail. Calling my dad was not a good option for me and calling him at 3 in the night could have affected his health. The only option I had was Nikith, but that too, seemed useless to me as college gates were closed at that time. Every employee was getting a chance to call one by one and it was my turn. They gave me my mobile and asked me to call, and at that moment I was in doubt and it was getting difficult for me to decide. I wanted to think and analyse the situation once again, but the constable shouted at me and asked me to make a call right then, or my chance was over. I called Nikith but he didn't pick the call. I tried his number 4 times but he didn't pick any call so my chance was wasted and they asked me to go back to the bench where we all were sitting. Luckily, Nikith called me back on my number.

"Yes Vihaan, what happened? Is everything alright?" He asked me in a sleepy voice.

"Nikith, I am in the police station right now. The Narcotics department raided our company for something illegal that I was not aware of. I lied about not knowing anything as I can't admit it in the police station because having info about crime is also a crime."

"Vihaan, tell me that you're pulling a prank with me," he replied.

"Please help me, Nikith," I begged him and dropped the call as my time was over.

I knew it was impossible for him to get out of college and I really didn't know how he would have helped me.

Calling him was way too risky at that time, because if he would have failed to help me, then after 24 hours, getting bail was impossible. Thanks to Nikith's dad, as he helped me to get out of that situation without any trouble. He had some contacts in the Delhi government, so, within an hour I was escorted to my college. That night, I made a special entry in college. When two policemen dropped me outside my hostel, students from every hostel were there to escort me to the room.

This incident increased my self-doubt on my potential as I had gotten myself into trouble once again. My dad was working extremely hard to earn money so that I could study properly, and here I was, creating more nuisance. I decided not to get involved in any kind of activity in future because every time I tried to do something good, I just ended up in some trouble.

I got fame in college after that, and everyone had a different perception about me. Some thought I was selling weed and hash and some thought I fell into the company's trap. There was also an internal inquiry in college as there was a warning notice from the police for me. College was not harsh on me as they understood my situation. In fact, they promised to offer me a full scholarship if I managed to get at least 90% in the second year. The promise was lucrative, but I knew my limitations. I took this opportunity as a motivation to score well.

Everything got normal in 2-3 days but I was still part of gossip within the whole college. In fact, I was part of my gossip, too. I narrated the whole incident around 100+ times to other students. I made that incident a bit spicy and crispy while narrating, to get more attention. I was trending till the mid semesters came. My stardom was gone after the exams as mid semesters were not to score marks but to realise that I was there for studies. I didn't score well in that because of my mental state. It was so difficult for me to focus on my books and thermodynamics made it more difficult for me to focus. Many suggested that I start drinking alcohol, but I resisted them. I didn't want to get into new trouble. Alcohol and drugs were a part of daily routine for many students. I already got in trouble because of it so I never thought of trying it.

I used to only talk to Nikith at that time. From the last few months, I hadn't contacted Rashi and her group. They called me multiple times and texted me, but I didn't reply back. I was helpless at that time and wanted to talk to someone, so I called Rashi to talk. I hadn't spoken to her for around 3 months and there wasn't any reason that I stopped talking to her.

"Hi Rashi, how are you?" I said after she picked the call.

"Hi Vihaan, I am good. You have been ignoring me for a long time and I don't think you need me. Now you are a famous personality in college," she replied in sarcasm.

I was expecting some sympathy from her but she was angry with me and she was absolutely right on her part. Without any hesitation I told her everything, including my imagination on DJ night.

"You are stupid, Vihaan. You should have told me about your feelings. I would have considered you. You are a nice person," she replied.

I wanted to act smart, so I replied "You can consider me now, too. My feelings are still there."

This forced her to share her secret relationship with Rathik. They were dating for a while, and on a trip, Rathik had proposed to her. No one knew about their relationship and I was the third person after them who knew about it then.

I called her so I could feel better, but after I came to know about it, I was totally lost. One by one, things were happening and it was directly affecting my studies and my mental health.

In the last 1 year, I worked more than anyone else but everyone was reaping the fruits of their hard work except me. It was like everyone was investing in the same option and doing the same trade, but except me, everyone was earning some profit out of it and I was losing my portfolio. Maybe, I was not predicting entry and exit positions correctly, or I was taking undercalculated risks expecting more returns.

That day, after having dinner in a mess, I went to my favourite spot in my college with my diary. I usually write about things that happened to me or about what I should have done to prevent my problems. Every year, our college sees one suicide and I didn't want to be that person. While I was writing, Nikith came to me. He never disturbed or interrupted me while I wrote my diary, but that day, he knew I wanted someone to be with me.

"Vihaan, can I ask you something?" Nikith tapped on my shoulder and asked.

"Oh, Nikith! I thought you slept. By the way, what brings you here?" I asked him back.

"I know you are writing your diary but I think you need a living being right now who can listen to you and guide you. I wanted to be that living being, so here I am," he replied.

"You know, for the first time, I wrote a poem. Would you like to hear it?" I asked.

Without hesitation, he asked me to recite it. I called that security guard also and asked him to sit and listen to my poem. It was my first open mic with two people in the audience.

"Please listen carefully and tell me how it is," I asked them and started reciting.

"Pehle kahi janay ke liye rasta khud dhundte
Ya rastay mein logon se puchte
Par ab Google maps ne aasan kar diya hai
Bas usko apni manzil batani hoti hai
Raah apne aap dikha deta hai

Main bhi Google ke bharosay ek safar par nikal gaya
Rasta nahi pata tha toh maine bhj manzil daal di
Uss manzil ka naam tha success
Par wahan pahuchne ki guarantee nahi di Google ne
Google dikha raha tha ye manzil 20-30 saal dur hai
Itna time dekh kar main 10-12 saal toh sota raha
Jab aankh khuli toh rasta bheed ke karan re-route
ho gaya

Gaadi par fast tag nahi tha toh Toll gate par jurmana bhi dena pada
Jurmana apno ka tha
Kyuki iss safar mein paise kahi kaam nahi aate.

Jaise jaise Toll aa rahe the
Saath mein log kam hotay ja rahe the

Ek jagah toh aisa laga ke wapas hi chala jata hu
Par uss mod par wapsi jaana namunkin tha
Beech mein kayi baar thak kar aaram kar leta tha
Par gaadi nahi ruki
Kyon ki gaadi papa chala rahe the
Aur petrol ka zimma mummy par tha

Jab nikla tha tab socha rasta aasan hoga
Par ek jagah toh aisi aayi ke wahan gaadi bhi nahi ja sakti thi
Toh akele hi apna bojh lekar badhna tha
Peeche har koi keh raha tha wahan pahuch kar bahut acha lagega
Abhi main pahucha bhi nahi aur akela sa lag raha hai

Google ne bhi saath chod diya hai ab
Kyuki network nahi aate na

Kuch log mil jate hain raste mein
Magar vo bhi thakay nazar aatay hai

Ek baat sahi hai yahan
Manzil na mili toh chaaro taraf khaai hai
Neechay dekhta hu toh kankaal nazar aatay hai
Shayad unko bhi manzil nahi mili

Ab har kadam par sochta hu ke location alag daal deta
Toh kya hota kahi ja nahi pata par apno ke beech mar toh pata
Apno ke beech mar toh pata"

After I ended, I could hear applause from both of them. The way they appreciated it, my confidence was at a new level.

"Good one, poet Vihaan. It was really good. You should try doing open mics," Nikith said while applauding.

"Maybe the stage can help you to solve your problems. I have some contacts who conduct open mics in different colleges and cafes, so I will ask them to give you a chance. Also, it is too late now, come and sleep," Nikith said and left the room.

I wanted to give a try to what Nikith said, and before implementing, I ran my analysis. All my past experience was saying that I should not put my leg in this, but failure was directly proportional to the fact whether I followed Nikith's advice or not, so I asked Nikith to count me in. After that, it was the beginning of a new me. I started doing open mics regularly after that, and it really helped me to improve my mental health. For the rest of the second year in college, I studied and did open mics, and by the end of year I improved myself in studies as well, so it was a comeback for me. Apart from studies, it helped me overcome Rashi's incident and we became friends again. I accepted my fate. With a little bit of improvement in my life, I was getting closer to fulfilling my mom's dream, too.

"Roz savere uth kar
Apne aap ko darpan ke dusri aur dekh kar
thoda darr jata hu
Thoda sehem kar nazro se nazray milane ke
koshish karta hu
Ussi waqt apne aap se haar jata hu

Har din apne aap se
Uss dar ka karan
Uss sharmindagi ki wajeh
Aur
Uss haar ka matlab jaanney ke koshish karta hu

Vo koshish koshish hi reh jaati hai
Kyuki Maa mujhe kamiya nikalne nahi deti
Papa kabhi neechay girne nahi dete
Aur mera ehem jhukne nahi deta

Kal shayad naya savera hoga
Jab main darr kar bhi himmat juta paunga
Uss haar ko jeet mein badal paunga
Aur duniya ki nazro mein amar ho jaunga
Amar ho jaunga"

"Desire and anger, born from passion, are endless and dangerous. Only when we let go can we truly move forward."

Chapter 9

Day 1 Stumps (Present)

"I am sorry for your loss, Vihaan. I know it is not easy to overcome the pain of losing a mother. I am a grownup, and I was also broken when I lost my mother last month. And Vihaan, you are a good writer, I believe. You explained the journey of your whole life in a single poem, but I am still confused why after every failure, you want to die or have such bad thoughts."

I took a glass of water because my lips and mouth got dry after narrating the story, and replied "Thank you sir, but I think everyone is not capable of handling pain. I am emotionally weak."

"I don't think you are weak. You just stick to your past and you don't put effort into forgetting things. Are you still in love with Rashi?"

I was silent when he asked about Rashi and again took a glass of water to ignore the question.

"You have answered my question. You can call it true love, but I will label it stupidity."

He stood up from the chair and closed his eyes and said "Chapter 3, Verse 37,

kaama eshha krodha eshha rajogunasamud bhavah |
mahaashano mahaapaapma viddhyenamiha vairinamh ||"

For a minute, I was in shock as I failed to understand the meaning of it. "Sir, it felt good when you said those lines, but can you explain the meaning?"

"Desire and anger which are born out of passion are insatiable, and prompt man to great sin and should be recognised as enemies. In times of change, desire and/or anger are born out of a sense of attachment. Dispassion and detachment may help one accept changes and tread on in life."

I had no words to reply to him back because that verse of Bhagavad Gita was written for me only. It was 5 in the evening and we both were tired. I didn't have enough energy to continue my story but I had no choice but to start narrating as I was at this side of the table.

"Vihaan, I am tired now, and if you continue, then I won't be able to digest anything. So shall we continue tomorrow at 10 in the morning?" He asked me.

It seemed like God was listening to me. I agreed and started keeping all my diaries in the bag. I left his house within 5 minutes and went to the Ganga Ghat. I was not in the mood of going home because I didn't want to get emotional and change my mind. My father didn't know about my whereabouts. He thinks that I am in Delhi, doing my job. My friends think that I am at home and preparing for my masters. Whenever my dad calls me, I have to build some imaginary story about my college. According to that story, my boss is a bit cranky and there are 7 people in my team. Also, I got a promotion last week because that day my dad was feeling low, so to boost his emotions I self-promoted myself. Nikith always asks me about my performance in thermodynamics and like every time, I tell him how good I am doing in every subject except thermodynamics and the verbal section. The reality was way too different from what they had in their minds. For the last few weeks, I have been dependent on a nearby temple for food as I had to save my money for admission in that building.

I spent the whole night near the ghat. I was not in the mood to sleep as I had to complete my letter for my dear ones, but I slept because my body was tired. That guy was praying at that ghat in the morning and I saw him reciting prayers. After he left, I took a bath in the river and went towards his house. This time he didn't do any formality and he directly called me to the room. I was hoping that he would offer me breakfast, and in that hope, I didn't eat anything in the morning.

When I entered the room, I recited

"Chapter 2, Verse 63

krodhaadbhavati sammoha sammohaatsmritivibhramah |
smritibhramshaadbuddhinaasho buddhinaashaat
pranashyati ||"

He looked at me and asked “Do you know what you said? I think you are contradicting yourself now.”

“I know the meaning of it, Sir.

Anger leads to clouding of judgment, which results in bewilderment of the memory. When the memory is bewildered, the intellect gets hazy; and when the intellect is vague, one is ruined.

I knew this explains the reason for my desire to get in there again. After I left, I thought about my decision and there is a lot to do in my life but for that I should have the will to do anything except it. I don’t want to build more stories for my dad and my friends. So shall I continue?”

He got silent. I think he was able to see my pain through my eyes. He offered me the glass of water as there were tears in my eyes and asked me to take my time before I continue my story. I refused water and without wasting even a second, I took my diary and started from where I had left...

"You know it's the end when you've lost everything, and the weight of trying to start over feels too heavy to bear."

Chapter 10

Counterfeiting

Things were moving at a lightning pace. The pain of losing mom was still fresh, like she had died yesterday, but it was already her death anniversary. I had no plans to go home after second year, as in Delhi I felt my mom was still alive, but at home my mind had to face that reality. My dad asked me to come for a few days and I couldn't refuse him as he made me emotional about my mom. After completing the rituals, I packed my bag and came to Delhi. Nikith, Rathik, and I took a special permission from the hostel warden for a room so that we could implement Nikith's idea. It had been a year that Nikith was planning some or the other thing for the third year.

He was planning to open a small company, or as you can say, a start-up. From 1980-2005, there was an industrial revolution in our country, and after that, there was a boom of start-ups. In our college, only 50+ start-ups were running at a small scale. In India, the number of start-ups is equal to the number of sweet shops. All three of us had an average life. None of us had done something exceptional or brilliant. We took science, as it was in demand. We got into B.Tech for the same reason, and now it was time for a start-up.

The idea of a start-up was so common that if you gathered 100 people, 30-40 of those must be doing the same thing. The idea was printing customised goods for college societies, fest teams and some of the corporate clients. We named our start-up The Campus Bazaar as we were dealing within our campus only. Without any legal formalities, we started our business. In reality, we were just the mediator between the manufacturer and societies. It was not a unique idea but it was good enough to earn a decent amount. All three of us had a different approach for the start-up. I wanted to earn money for my personal expenditure, Nikith wanted to gain some experience for MBA, and Rathik wanted it for experience in the non-technical field for placements. So, neither of us was thinking of making this start-up unicorn.

He explained his idea, and without any doubt, I agreed to be a part of it. It was the first time that the three of us were part of the same thing, and I had confidence in Nikith. Before implementing anything, we had to do some research work. Research work included the types of items and its quality that can be printed and a vendor from where we can have things at a decent price. That was basically field research, and in Delhi, the best place to find vendors was Shidipura, which was near Karol Bagh. In that particular area, there were around 300+ vendors and we visited every shop. To cover all shops, Nikith and

I divided the area and approached them for samples and price lists. Nikith was good at the communication part so he got some 48 quotations from 150 shops, and I managed to get only 5. Rathik was given special exemption from that field work because it was Rashi's friend's birthday so he had to be there. We thought the task was easy because after getting a quotation we just had to analyse them on the basis of parameters like price & quality. To make it look professional, we did some easy analysis on excel. We just sorted the price list from low to high and quality from high to low. This was the difference between start-up and business. For start-ups, you need to use some fancy words and some technology.

On our first day of the third year, we got our first order. It was a small order of 15 T-shirts only. We calculated our cost and quoted them after adding 20% to the cost. Rathik and Nikith decided to give 100% of the profit to me as they just wanted to gain some experience and my financial condition was not good. And they got ready to bear the loss if it was there. But there was one condition, that I had to manage all operational work including delivering the product to customers. For the sake of money, I accepted this deal without knowing the consequences.

They both started approaching clients for orders and converting them. And I had to coordinate with vendors for orders and keep a check that products are printed as they have demanded. My job was hectic. For every order I had to travel to Karol Bagh to place the order and to pick it up for delivery. There was a special budget for delivery which the client paid, and in that budget, I had to travel there twice. Usually, I used to go alone to deliver the product, but when the order was big enough for a single person, then one of them used to help me. Delivery fees we took from clients was 200 rupees, so to save money from delivery charges, I started travelling via bus, as the tickets varied from 10-15 rupees per side, so by putting extra effort, I started saving a decent amount. I never told them the amount I am spending on delivering the product, and they never asked me.

In the first month of business, I earned 2000 bucks, and with time, the number of orders and quantity was increasing. In some orders, we lost some money as we failed to satisfy customers, but our overall portfolio was in the green. In our fifth semester, our total profit was fifty thousand rupees, which, including my profit from travelling allowance, went up to fifty -eight thousand rupees. But the financial gains led to the drop in my grades and studies. I spent the majority of my time travelling to and from college to Karol Bagh. I spent more hours on roads and in Karol Bagh than I spent in college. They both had enough time to study and prepare for placements and I was busy filling my pocket. They also gained some skills in converting orders and handling customers and I just learnt some labour skills like screen printing and carrying weight on shoulders while travelling. For all those things and time, I was not worried about that. Instead, in December, I stayed in college. My aim was to save enough money so that I could submit my fourth-year fees on my own and rent for 6 months for a flat that I will take after getting a job. The plan was clear and ready to be implemented. In the months of February and March, I was able to achieve my targets because the demand was raised by 100% due to the festive season in colleges. After that, Nikith and Rathik decided to quit the start-up as they gained whatever they wanted to, but that same day, we got a big order from our college admin. The order was so big that profit from one particular order was equivalent to the profit we earned in 7-8 months. For this type of order, I needed them, hence I offered them equal division of profit in a particular order. For one last time, we started working for an order. The advance which we got from college was enough to bear the cost and the amount on delivery was supposed to be our profit.

We didn't have any legal documentation complete, so in accordance with the law, we couldn't produce a legal bill. Usually, college societies don't require any bill for purchase so we didn't face any issue, but to withdraw payment from college admin, we had to submit bills in the name of college. Getting a proper bill was a challenging task for us. Rathik was used to it as he was a society head in which he had used fake bills to withdraw the money. So, for that order, he took the charge to arrange a legit bill and we both got into delivering the products on time. The products were delivered on time with a bill which completely looked legal to us. Only Rathik knew that it had a fake GST number with a fake company name which didn't exist. The order incharge in the college file was me, so I was the one who signed that bill and went to the accounts department. It generally takes 9-10 days to process the payment but we got a call from the accounts section on the 4th day only.

"Are you Vihaan Miglani?" the Accounts officer asked me with a bill in his hands.

"Yes sir, I am Vihaan. Is my cheque ready?" I asked eagerly.

"Where have you got this bill from?" He asked and turned the bill towards me.

"Sir, it is from the vendor from where we outsourced this order. Is everything fine?"

"I am sending this file to the Dean of this college. He will see what needs to be done now. This bill is totally fake. The GST number is not real. Now there will be an inquiry on you for generating a fake bill," he replied.

I was shocked after I came to know the reality. I called Nikith urgently because the situation was out of control. My records in college were not good, as in second year-I was caught in a raid, and now this. Nikith was with me every time and he even accepted in front of the dean that he was part of that order, but Rathik refused so that he could be safe from punishment. That day, I realised that Vibhishana did wrong with his brother Ravana. I was betrayed by my dearest friend. I wanted to beat him right at the moment when he claimed that he was unaware of that order and bill, but he was right at his spot. He helped me realize that sometimes we need to be selfish if we are not wrong and the situation is not in our favour.

The whole inquiry ended in 6-7 days and my dad was also called to be part of it. Instead of supporting me, my dad scolded me for the act which I didn't commit. They were punishing me with a rustication letter, but they settled with a 2 months suspension and Rupees 25,000 penalty on me and Nikith, as my dad started begging in front of the Dean when he told him about rustication. We were not allowed to stay in a hostel for those two months so I went back home with my father. Nikith also joined us as he didn't have a place to live.

It was the last day when we both spoke to Rathik, because he got us into a big trouble and left us alone. In that incident, I just lost everything I had. My friend, part of the money I earned, and trust of my dad. It is easy to lose trust but hard to gain it back. For the time, when me and Nikith were at home, he didn't speak even once.

"Nikith, you know I haven't done anything wrong. It was not my fault," I said and started crying.

"If my dad would have been there, he would have reacted in the same way as yours. Just stay calm and he will forgive you soon. Start your preparation for the placement session which is only 4 months away. By the way, you should hand over all the money you have earned to your dad. He must be proud.".

I took all my money from the locker, which was around 1.6 lakh rupees, and kept it in my father's workspace.

"Dad, please take this money. I earned it last year from the start-up." I kept a bundle of notes and started waiting for a reply from him. He took 5 minutes and said "You can keep your money with you. I don't want stolen money, earned by doing such misdeeds."

Without wasting a second, I packed my bag and left for Delhi with Nikith. I didn't want to stay with him even for a moment. I came back to my hostel and straight away went to Rathik's room.

"Now I am an orphan. My mom has died and dad is not talking to me just because of you," I said in a loud voice and started beating him with a stick. He knew he made a mistake back then so he didn't do anything in self-defence. After I stopped, he said, "I am sorry Vihaan, I am really sorry. I got scared at that moment. So, I did what I felt was right. I know I cannot ask for an apology but I am ready to bear the punishment for the sin I did."

He called my dad in front of me and told him everything he should have told him earlier. My dad spoke to me after he came to know the truth. It was the happiest moment for me. He apologized for his behaviour but still sounded strict. He asked me to get a good placement if I wanted him to forgive me.

That incident was the end of my happy days streak and I didn't know what was coming next. I forgave Rathik after realising that I would have done the same and I asked him to help me in preparing for placement in exchange.

The last phase of my college was about to start and I had to give my best so that I could prove my abilities to my father and my mom who sacrificed her life for me.

"Acceptance is finding peace in your failures, knowing that sometimes, it's okay to feel like it's the end."

Chapter 11

Hunting

As the fourth and the final year started, we all got into preparation mode. It was like we all were preparing for JEE once again. The competition was so high that to beat others you had to study for hours. I got all the study material which was required to clear the interview and with that I started working on my resume. Building a resume was the toughest part of the preparation as it was the first thing which a company sees, and you get a chance for an interview if you get shortlisted on the basis of resume. I still remember the day in my first year when I saw fourth year students in formal dress near the placement cell. It is always easy to be on the other side of the problem as you just can see the problem and not face it.

In accordance with our college guidelines, the placement session marked its inception from 1st Jan in last semester, but that year they decided to follow a new pattern. In that pattern, there was no fixed period for the session and companies would come to the campus according to their availability. This new practice was introduced to increase the number of companies visiting the campus. I already had wasted my third year in that start-up and hadn't prepared anything for placement. The number of regrets in my life were more than the number of companies visiting our campus every year. That new rule increased pressure on me, as according to it, placements were supposed to start in mid-september and after that I had only 2 months to prepare. I was starting a marathon when everyone was already on second or the third round, so to make it to the finish line on time, I had to sprint.

Everyone was helping me to prepare for it. Rashi and Nikith were putting more effort than me in my preparation. There is a proverb that says: Dog's tail can never be straight, and I was the dog's tail from that proverb. With so much pressure and numerous reasons to prove myself, I should have worked harder, but instead of preparing, I invested all my time sleeping. My attitude of being lazy still persisted. After all that happened in those four years, I didn't change my attitude. I watched 3 idiots every alternate day for four months. I thought it would help in clearing the interview, similar to Raju Rastogi. Yes, I was Raju Rastogi from that movie, and Nikith was Rancho. There was some mismatch in Farhan's and Rathik's behaviour and lifestyle but he had no choice but to be Farhan to complete our 3 idiots script. As days were approaching, my sleep hours also increased. Nikith used to scold me every single day but it was of no use. Like I said earlier, I was the dog's tail and that can never be straight. The way Nikith was preparing for his MBA exam, I was confident that he would crack it.

In a placement session, there are a minimum of 3 rounds in every process. Screening is done on the basis of the resume, and after screening you need to pass an aptitude test and then the final interview. So, for securing a job, one must be good in all three. For every type of round there is a different preparation mode, and for interviews, everyone was going through mock interview sessions and I was doing only 10% of what others were doing. I had self- realization, too, but there was no regret. I think I was preparing for my failure at that point, or I might have had confidence to achieve what I wanted to. It is easier to think theoretically than facing things practically.

I messed up my mid semesters, too, as placement preparation was priority at that time, and at the same time I didn't prepare for it. Every night I used to promise myself that I will double my efforts from the next day but it didn't happen.

I still remember the date when the first MNC visited our campus; it was 18th September. All were excited for it and everyone wanted to crack it because getting a job in the first company is an achievement itself. But on the other hand, I thought that it was the first company and I should focus on the process, not on being selected. I was not anticipating getting rejected in the Aptitude round. My résumé and thinking, according to me, were far superior than that of 50% of pupils, but that round made me realise that reality was not resonating with my thoughts. I still didn't have any regrets for not clearing the round but I was jealous of the fact that Rathik cleared all rounds in the first company and secured a job. It was the first company and 100+ companies were yet to visit so I had a lot of chances to prove myself. After getting rejected, I told everyone that the job profile is not good so it's okay for me.

I did the same after every rejection without realising the fact that I was not able to clear the aptitude test which was just the basic round. Till the time I realised that I needed more practice and skills for placement, I had already been rejected by 40-45 companies. Everyone was securing jobs around me, and I was stuck in aptitude. After every company, I lied to my dad because I didn't want to accept my mistake in front of him. He always believed what I said and he always motivated me for the next company.

It was February, and almost everyone was placed and students who wanted to go for further admissions were admitted to the college they wanted to. Nikith got admission in FMS college, One of the top colleges for MBA in India. And I was still wearing those same formals in the morning every day for placement, and came back to the hostel with the same news. Around mid-February, one company visited our college and only 10 students were appearing for it, including me. Everyone thought that I would get the placement that day. But after the test, the company selected 9 students for an interview and I was the only one who got rejected. According to me, I always got rejected by 1-2 marks, so I went to the placement coordinator for my marks in the test. After seeing it, I realised that I was living in a delusional state till date. I would have gotten negative marks had they followed the JEE pattern.

While I was struggling with clearing the first round, everyone was busy going on trips, parties and planning for farewell. My dad also knew that my final year was about to end so he got worried. One day, I called him and pretended that I had got a placement in Delhi's company. I didn't want to lie to him but that was the only option. I was in a position to lie to my dad but I couldn't lie to my mom. She was seeing me from the skies and she must have been disappointed with me. Late realisation of my failure led me to depression. The pressure on my head was increasing day by day and apologizing to my mom became part of my daily routine.

As expected, I was unplaced till the last day of college. Everyone was emotional about leaving college and friends behind and they all had plans for the farewell night. But I was going towards depression and my mental health was deteriorating day by day. It felt like I had wasted 6 years of my life, including 11th and 12th class, and wasted all the sacrifices my mom and dad made, so that I could do well in my career.

Finally, on the day of farewell, I decided that I will go to Mukti Bhawan in Varanasi, as I wanted to end my life cycle. Suicide was a good option for me at that point in time, but committing suicide would not have end my pain.

I wrote a poem that day itself and decided to do my last open mic in college. My poems were the only part left in my identity. Everyone thought that I am a good writer, but the truth was, everything I wrote was part of my life. A good writer is the one who can write on any topic he wants to. No one refused my request to open the mic on farewell night. Everyone was dressed up properly, girls were in sarees and boys were wearing coats, pants and tuxedos. I knew I was seeing everyone for the last time as

I had different plans. Everyone was clicking pictures as a memory and making some promises with each other. I was also part of that promise, knowing the fact that my promise of staying in touch and visiting Chennai to Nikith's house is a false one, but at that time I made that promise. Everyone was in the happy zone till my open mic began.

"Hello everyone, some of you know me and for some I am just a stranger, but today it doesn't matter. We all are leaving this place to start a new journey. Some of you have got your dream jobs and the rest must have got admission in higher studies. But I am jobless and hopeless, I don't have any idea what I will do from tomorrow, but today, I know what I am doing. I have written a poem based on some incidents and my thoughts. This poem can be my last poem. Because I might resign today." I addressed the audience. It was a demotivating introduction for them and the crowd got silent when I told them about resigning. They must be thinking that I am committing suicide.

I broke the silence and said "I am not committing suicide, stay calm guys. I would have done it earlier if I had to. So, listen to my poem, and if you appreciate it, you may applaud after I finish."

Zindagi ki Kitab

Har roz subha
Sabse upar wali shelf se apni zindagi ke kitaab
utha leta hu
Aur har roz uspar se ek dhul ke moti parat ko hata
kar kholta hu.

Vo kitaab mein ek naya panna khol kar ghanto
betha rehta hu
Jo pen hai usmay syahi toh puri hai par bahut
atak kar chalta hai
Ghanto ghanto chidkta hu tab ja kar ek shabd
likh pata hu.

Jab lagta hai ke pata hai aage kya likhna hai
Tabhi ek hawa ka jhoka
Pannay palat deta hai
Aur main sab chod kar usko dekhne lag jata hu

Shuru ke panne bahut hi saaf likhawat mein hai aur
galtiya naa ke barabar hai
Shayad vo pannay papa mummy ne likhay hongay.
Aur jaise hi main aage badhta hu toh likhavat
gandi hoti rehti hai
Seedhi lakiray tedi hoti hai aur likha toh bahut
kuch hua hai par uska matlab nahi hai.

Aakhir ke kuch panne toh aise hai jaise koi paheli ho
Jisko main khud hi samajh nahi pata

Aur jab likhavat doctors ke writing se bekaar ho jaati
hai tab main usko patak kar band kar deta hu.
Fir thode soch vichaar ke baad unn khaali panno ko
dekhne lag jata hu jo aanay wale samay mein bharne hai
Wahan ek sapno ka mahal banata hu
Aur kuch samay baad uss panne ko faad deta hu
Thak haar kar vo kitab wapas ussi jagh rakh deta hu
Fir uss upar wale ko kosta hu jisnay ye kitab di hai.

Har roz ki tareh apni khuli aankhon ko band kar apne
aap se vada krta hu kal isko pura karunga aur so jata hu.

I got a standing ovation from the crowd for the poem. It was my best open mic as everyone listened to me carefully and I was able to see in some of the audience that they were relating to it. While reciting the poem, I saw Rashi sitting in the front row. She was looking beautiful, wearing a black saree with a backless top. Her hair was straight and kajal on her eyes was an added point to her beauty. After I finished my show, I went to her so that I could talk to her one last time. As I approached her, she hugged me tightly and said "I know, Vihaan, you have faced a lot and we were not with you in your tough times. I know you will not give up so easily. You will get a better job than anyone in college." I hugged her back and apologized for my behaviour. I apologized to everyone for my mistakes and behaviour because I didn't want to regret it later. I clicked a picture of me, Rashi, Nikith and Rathik with Nikith's instant camera for a memory, as they were with me every time. Rathik was still apologizing for that GST bill. I already forgave him for his mistakes because he was with me in tough times and also gave his percentage of profit to me. Everyone deserves a second chance.

After the farewell ended, we went up to the hostel room to pack our bags as the next day we had to leave the college. All three of us stayed together that night and were sharing memories with each other. For the first time I was seeing Nikith so emotional. He got some personalised gifts for both of us. That night I thought about everything that happened to me in four years. If I look back into the past, there was a lot that needed to be corrected, but time travel is still just a theory for humans.

The next morning, we all had tears in our eyes. Everyone must be sad about leaving the place as it has given a lot to them, but I was leaving in regret because I was not able to achieve anything with the opportunity that college gave me. I had only eighty thousand at that time, and I couldn't have come home because my dad would have got to know about my placement, and in that budget staying in Delhi was difficult. So, I took a bus to Varanasi but I didn't go home. I went directly to Mukti Bhawan.

"Hope is believing that there's a way out of the cycle of life, and sometimes, it's the only thing that makes the journey worthwhile."

Chapter 12

15 Day Notice Period

"Sir, this was my whole story with reasons why I wanted to get back there. As you can see, I have no reason to live for my dreams. I don't have enough willpower to work for anything now. I just want salvation."

During the last two chapters, his eyes were closed and I was in doubt whether he was listening to me or not. He was tapping his finger on the table constantly which gave me some confidence. After I told him about the completion of my story, he opened his eyes and said, "Vihaan I heard your story from the beginning. Should I brief it to you so that you can tell me whether I have understood everything or not?"

He was asking for permission and then he started briefing me my story without my consent

"You were a bright student till 12th class, as clearing that exam is not easy. You were getting a better college but you refused it because of financial conditions. Not everyone can afford such an amount so you got more than what you could afford according to your dad's income. Then, in college, your mind got diverted into 100 other things, including a girl. You continuously tried to do things which could improve your life but you never succeeded according to you, and after you started losing people from your life, you just gave hope and instead of putting in more effort, you became reckless and accepted your defeat. This is the conclusion of your whole story, right?" He asked.

"Yes sir," I replied.

"Can you tell me why you didn't commit suicide? It is an easy task for you, I believe, or you didn't want to work for that also?"

"Sir, there is a difference between dying and getting salvation. I would have committed suicide, but then I will get another life after my death. I want to end my life cycle and never wish to be back here as any form of life. I was born in Varanasi, and according to our mythology, Varanasi is a place where you can get salvation if you die here."

He stood from his chair and went towards his bookshelf to take some books and while opening its pages he said, "Vihaan, my name is Manbudh Das Tripathi. My ancestors opened Mumukshu Bhawan in 1920 for old people. They can live there as much as they want, but only 15 days for people below 60. I am the director of that Bhawan."

He started reading lines from a book "For the soul, there is neither birth nor death at any time. It has not come into being, does not come into being, and will not come into being. It is unborn, eternal, ever-existing, and primeval. It is not slain when the body is slain."

"Your soul can never die. Your body is just a way for the soul to fulfil your task. But you said it correctly. If you die here in Varanasi, your soul will never enter any body again and you will attain salvation forever."

I was totally shocked when he told me that he was the director. I stood up from my chair and held his feet and started begging him to get salvation.

"Vihaan, there is a difference in what you think, and the real purpose of that place. You are willing to die. Your priority is not salvation. I think this must be the reason that you failed the first time," he said.

"Sir, I know, but at that place, I can directly ask God to take away my soul from this world. That place is a one-way gate for the soul, hence, to fulfil my purpose, I need to go there," I replied to him.

"You can ask God from any other place. My ancestors opened that hotel so that people who think that their end is near or they are ready to leave the materialistic world can leave everything and can live there until they die. Salvation is not only to die. It can be different for everyone. If you forget everything from the past and decide to move on in life, then it can be a nirvana for you."

"There are a lot of people in your life who will be shocked when they come to know about your decision. Have you told anyone about it?" He asked.

"No sir, I have lied to everyone. I have told my college friends Nikith, Rathik, and Rashi that I am at home and preparing for my masters exam and I told my dad that I am working as I told you in the story. They will be hurt if I die here, but I am already prepared for it," I said and joined my hands before him and again started begging for one chance to be in the bhawan. He kept his hand on my shoulder and asked me to get up. He wiped off my tears and said "Your body and mind are so young right now and you have a lot in front of you to achieve, but when I heard your story, I understood why you don't want to live anymore. If I compare your problem with others, then your problem may be small for some and huge for others. Problems are relative for everyone, so I won't say that your problem is small. You failed multiple times and the reason for failure was not you. I think God, or you can say, your creator, wanted you to work harder to achieve your goals and dreams. You must have seen people around you who achieve things easily. According to our mythology, everyone has to face problems written for them by the creator and everyone will get what they deserve. Not everyone can be Ambani or Elon Musk; some have to be a beggar so that there is balance in the universe.

In your life, you put effort in various fields but you gave up easily on everything you did, and you want to end your life here. I haven't heard of you having so much dedication for any other work. You have been waiting to get into Mumukshu Bhawan for the last 50 days and you put so much effort into narrating your story. I would like to give you a second chance. You have 15 days, if you attain salvation, then it is okay, otherwise you have to continue your life ahead and do what needs to be done for survival. Okay?"

His every word was meaningful, and I was calm after listening to him. I agreed to all his conditions and was ready to move in there for one last time.

"Nothing in life comes easy; even death demands pain."

Chapter 13

Bhavan

The holy city of Varanasi in India's northern state of Uttar Pradesh is the gateway to salvation, so goes a Hindu belief. Fuelled by such faith, thousands over the last centuries have travelled to Varanasi, also called Kashi, with a desire to die there. Dying in Varanasi is supposed to break the cycle of death and rebirth. Once one dies in Varanasi, he or she is never reborn, and thus attains salvation. In Varanasi, death is not mourned but considered a blessing. To house those wanting to die, all sorts of hotels and lodging have sprung up over the years. One such place is the Mumukshu Bhawan (Home for the Ailing) also known as Moksha Bhawan, which means Salvation Home, which was established in 1920. Mumukshu charges minimal rent for accommodation and electricity. Those who cannot afford it are also allowed to stay. More than 300 people stay in Mumukshu and most of them are above 60. They come here to die. In a year, we get around 800 people from around the country who come to spend their last days in Kashi. Some Non-Residential

Indians, too, have come. On average, people are allowed to stay for 15 days. For some, it could be two or three days or even a month till they die. For younger people, 15 days are maximum and according to their rules, they can't get in there if they fail to die in those 15 days.

Yet again, I was ready to get in there. I packed my bag, kept diaries inside, and left Manbudh Das Tripathi's house with a letter of admission. It was the first interview of my life and I think I got a chance just because of his kindness. Nikith told me once that cracking the first interview is really challenging. I wanted to tell him that I had finally done it, but I couldn't. After getting a chance, I was in a little doubt because Manbudh told me so many things about life, but I decided to stay with my decision. I took a rickshaw from his house to Mumukshu Bhawan. It was not too far from there but there is a spot from where you have to go on walking, as no means of transport can go there. That Bhawan was located near the Ganga ghat, so the paths were not strong enough to hold the weight of vehicles. As I walked towards the Bhawan, the old people and babas were staring at me as I was 1/3rd the age of the people there.

I kept my bag on the floor and looked at the gate. The gate was made of wood and was unpainted, handles made of iron with some rust on it. Just above the gate, there was an old board on which was written "Mumukshu Bhawan - Way to Salvation". I opened the gate with 1.5 times the force required to open a normal gate. The place was the same as it was 50 days ago. Water was dripping from the roof of that room. People say that it has been years that no one has fixed that hole on the roof. As I took my first step inside that room, one old guy said "Welcome, son,

Manbudh sir told us about you. Have a seat there, our doctor will first check you before you start your journey."

Everyone has to pass the medical test because they don't allow people with diseases to get in. According to them, cancer patients are the one who are already blessed with death and they don't need to stay there. The front room which is a reception had two doors; the second door was the door to salvation, or you can say the bhawan. After I passed these tests, I picked my luggage and started following the caretaker. Just after the room, there was a huge open space with a banyan tree in the middle where people could sit. On the left side, there was a space for a garden, and on the right side, there were stairs to the ganga ghat. The view on the right side was similar to the baga beach view. It was fully filled with people standing with water level up to their knees. Men were shirtless and women wore sarees. The only difference with the beach was that their people were for the last rituals for their loved ones.

The old uncle named Harish Lal Mehta was still there. He was sitting in the garden with a Bhagavad Gita in his hand. He recognized me and I greeted him back by joining my hands. After that open space ended, there was a building which had around 300 rooms. The area of that building was too less according to the number of rooms in it. The passage width was 1.5 times that of an average human being. Just before the building gate, there was a hall at the left side which was attached to it. That hall was for a place where people can go and pray to god without disturbance. That place was built unplanned, with poorly maintained architecture.

I was allotted room number 124, which was the same as my hostel's room number in the first year of college. I would have found a way to my room myself, but there was no logic in room numbers. 101 was on the second floor and 124 was on the third floor, and just next to 124 was 267. I followed that caretaker. It was a better option than getting lost in the building. That room was similar to room number 23, which was allotted to me the first time I was here. Its window was also broken and the bed size was 2 inches less than my height. The room looked like some part of a historical monument. It looked that old. There was just one bed and in reality, it was just a piece of wood. There was nothing like a bed and one almirah made of brick at the end of the room. With such facilities, it was insane that I was looking for an attached bathroom. The pain on the wall was improper and due to it, the room was looking dull like my life.

The last time, I had bought 7-8 dozen packets of Maggi because there was no food service in the bhawan. You have to make a meal yourself and Maggi was the only edible thing that I could make. The second time I didn't want to make any mistakes so I got some raw food like rice, dals, pulses and some flour so that I can cook my own food.

I cleaned my room properly and set up things accordingly. I took my t-shirt out of my bag and covered the window with it. I replaced the bulb of that room with a new one and marked 15 lines on the wall just next to the bed. 15 lines for 15 days.

This time I wanted to follow all the rules and regulations and the schedule given by them. Mobile phones were allowed, but I submitted them in the locker room to avoid disturbance. I texted my dad that I will be travelling for 15 days, owing to a project.

After submitting my phone, I went to Harish Lal Mehta to ask for the daily schedule. The session was not documented somewhere so he just told me verbally.

At 7 a.m. - Pooja in the hall.

At 8 a.m. - Yoga session near Ghat of ganga

At 10 a.m. - Cremation time if any person attains salvation

At 5 p.m. - Havan in the hall

At 6 p.m. - Aarti at Ganga Ghat

There were fixed timings for all these sessions and it was not mandatory to attend any of that. You have to volunteer yourself. During my first time there, I didn't attend any of that. I just spent 15 days in my room. It was more like a quarantine period for me.

I started preparing myself mentally for my first day, and set an alarm for 4 o'clock in the morning and kept my clothes for tomorrow on the table. I was so excited to wake up tomorrow on time and follow my planned schedule, that whole night I was just turning my side from one to another. Instead of waking up on time, I didn't sleep. Without any sleep, I got up from my bed to follow my schedule. I took my clothes and went to Ganga Ghat, my eyes were half closed as I was sleep deprived. The sky was a little blue and purple as it was time for sunrise, and I took a bath before the first ray of sun. After taking a bath, I felt cold as the water was chilled and there was a slight cool breeze.

Ignoring the fact that it can affect my health, I went to the hall for Pooja. After following all the daily morning sessions, I decided to go to the back side of the building.

Daily, from 10 a.m. to 4 p.m. we could see black smoke rising up from the backside of the building. I knew that there was a cremation ground there, but I never went there. The ground was a holy place for souls as the soul leaves the body and starts their journey to attain salvation. There was a small passage which led to the ground and that ground was divided in two parts. The side adjacent to Ganga Ghat was used to cremate bodies and the other side had a storehouse of woods used for cremation.

I went to the inquiry office to ask for some details.

“Hello sir, can you help me out?” I asked the old guy sitting on the counter.

“Yes, my son, how can I help you?” He replied in a sweet old voice.

“Sir, I am staying in Mumukshu Bhawan. I want to book one slot for myself. What are the charges?” I asked.

“There are two packages- for cremation we charge 10,000 rupees including charges of Pandit, and to perform all rituals of 17 days, we charge 25,000 rupees. But why do you want to die? I have never seen such a young person coming here.”

“Sir, I want to end my life. I am fed up with my life and I never want my soul to come back in any form of life. I hope I will get salvation here.”

"I think you don't know what salvation means. Hope this place helps you. If you want to book your slot, then you have to pay full in advance. We will return your money if you will not die."

"Sir, the charges are way too high for me. Can I get some discount?" I asked him.

"There is no discount, as we charge only the cost. There is no profit margin for us in that. There is one option for you. Take one axe from our store and you can cut wood on your own. We will not charge anything other than Pandit fees."

I agreed to it, but before cutting the wood I asked, "Can you tell me the amount of wood required for one dead body?"

"For one dead body you need 400-500 kg of wood, so you can cut any amount between it. It will be enough for you."

I thanked him, went to the labour room, took an axe from them and started the procedure of making my death bed. It was a beautiful moment as I was planning my last journey. If I would have died without giving any amount or preparing my own death bed, then they would have used their charity amount for my cremation or called my dad. With already so much burden on my shoulders, I didn't want any burden after my death. I decided to spend around 4-5 hours daily chopping the woods. On the first day I was only able to collect 30-35 kg of wood for myself, and according to that speed, it was impossible for me to finish the task on time.

On the first day itself, I was tired as I didn't sleep the whole night and ate only 1.5 meals a day. The food I cooked for myself was not even edible as it was half cooked. The calorie intake was much less than the basic requirement of my body, excluding the physical activities. My body dealt with it for one day and I was not sure till when my body could handle it. After completing my tasks on the first day, I was heading towards my room. I saw a guy sitting at Ganga Ghat, so I went towards him. It was 9 at night and the flow of Ganga was at maximum because of the full moon. As I approached him, I heard him whispering something in Hindi:

"Jai Shiv Omkara, Prabhu Jai Shiva Omkara,
Brahma, Vishnu, Sadashiv, Ardhangi Dhaara.
Om Jai Shiv Omkara
Ekanan Chaturanan Panchanan Raje,
Hansanan Garudaaan Vrishvaahan Saaje….."

He was reciting Shiva Aarti, so I turned my back as I didn't want to disturb him, but my footsteps were loud enough to grab his attention.

"Hi, Sir… my name is Vihaan Miglani."

"Hi, Vihaan." He stood up from his place and started packing the piece of cloth on which he was sitting. He was about to leave and I think I was the reason.

"Sorry sir, for disturbing you, but I got curious when I saw you sitting here at this time. May I know the reason?".

"After my body will be cremated, the ashes will be poured into this holy river, so I was praying for a better journey of my ashes. My soul will be in a better place after death, and just like soul, I want my body to be also at a better place. This body helped my soul to live as a human on planet Earth and human life is considered to be the most precious of all. According to the Vedas, there are 8.4 million species of life, and the conditioned soul is continuously passing through the different species according to his karma, under divine supervision. The Bhagavad Gita (2.22) says that just as one gives up an old shirt to put on a new one, the soul gives up an old body to acquire a new kind of body (*vasāmsi jirnāni yathā vihāya*). Thus, there are 8.4 million (84 lakh) types of bodies, out of which the soul assumes a body at the time of death. And the soul has to pass through all 8.4 million life forms to go into the human body. If I am giving a reward to my soul, then my body also deserves it."

I was stunned to know this information and felt ashamed that being from Varanasi, the holiest place of India, I didn't know anything about our culture and what our vedas say.

I felt stupid, yet asked him. "But why were you reciting Shiva's Aarti in front of Ganga?"

"I think you haven't read any mythological book." He kept all his stuff on the stairs and asked me to sit. It was dinner time, but we both were sitting at Ganga Ghat and talking about religion.

"If you look closely at Shiva's photograph, you will notice that Goddess Ganga is perched on his brow. The name Gangadhara is given to Shiva, and there is a story behind it. In ancient times, there was a king named Bhagiratha, who performed one thousand years of penance to please Lord Brahma for the river Ganga to come to Earth. He wished for the holy River Ganga to descend from the heaven to the Earth and free his 60,000 ancestors from the curse of Saint Kapila, for the dead to rise to heaven (this could only be accomplished through the offering of Niravapanjali (the Vedic rituals performed after death), which could only be accomplished through the offering of the sacred Ganga River, which was at the time in Heaven).

And after his successful penance, Ganga had to be released from heaven to Earth, but Lord Brahma said that no one could withstand the power of Ganga other than God Shiva. So, Shiva received Ganga in his matted locks (hair), and released her from his hair in seven streams, and thus became Gangadhara…. This is the reason why I was praying to Lord Shiva."

The amount of information was way too high for my processor to process and store in my database. It seems as though there are multiple hits of 504 on my server. At the same time, I realised that I haven't done anything in my life seriously. I have forgotten everything about 11th and 12th class and I didn't remember any chapter from my B.Tech. also. All I did was waste my time and resources. That uncle was able to see guilt in my eyes "Vihaan, I will not ask you why you are here. But is your soul ready to make this sacrifice?"

"What kind of sacrifice, sir?"

"Cremation is an important part of our view of destiny, embracing a symbolic form of the human embryo, which began with the male seed developing into bones and the female blood resulting in flesh. At the end of one's life, a reversal takes place as the heat of the funeral pyre divides flesh from bones. The flames of the cremation fire are the means by which the human form, or body, is presented to the gods as a last sacrifice. The spirit is released from the body for its journey, shaped by the individual's good (or karma) during his or her life."

With this kind of information, I was getting confused, and on the other hand I realised that death is also a journey. You have to go through many things and have to prepare yourself mentally to die.

Uncle knew I needed time to process everything he said, so he went to his room with all his stuff and I was sitting there just pondering over my life. It had been more than 24 hours that I hadn't slept and after that conversation my mind was in an excited state. I skipped my dinner as I was busy thinking about death, and at 11:30 p.m., I went to sleep.

Next day I got up on time again, followed my daily schedule and started searching for the uncle I met the previous day. After looking for one hour, I went to Harish Lal Mehta and asked, "Sir can you tell me the room number of that uncle who was sitting at Ganga Ghat last night."

"Which uncle are you talking about? Last night I only saw you. You were alone there," he replied.

I was scared when he said that and asked him again, "I was alone later on, but around 10, there was a guy with me. We were talking about the cremation process and was explaining to me the link between Ganga and Shiva."

"Oh, you must be talking about Girdhari Ji. He was fond of reading vedas and other mythology books and liked talking about everything he read, but his soul left this place 2 days ago. He used to reside in your room only, and he died on the day you came here. That's why we were able to allot you a room."

It seemed my heart stopped pumping for a while and there was darkness in front of my eyes. It was due to the shortage in supply of oxygen to my brain. I fainted. Everyone thought that I had attained the state of salvation, but unfortunately it was just a black out. After 20-25 minutes when I opened my eyes, I found myself in my room and Harish sir was standing at the door.

"Son, I think you were talking to his soul yesterday. There might be some hidden message in this for you. Don't be scared of what happened yesterday. There is no such thing as a ghost here. You just have to decode what happened yourself." He kept a bottle of Ganga Jal on my bed and left.

As soon as my body allowed me to stand on my feet again, I went directly to the cremation ground to cut wood for my death bed. If this thing would have happened to me at home or in college, I would have left that place. I can't live in a haunted place, but I took it as a hint from God. He must be trying to tell me the purpose and process of death. After completing my daily task at the cremation ground, I went to a library of Hindu Vedas and picked books about salvation and death.

There was an article in a book talking about salvation in Hinduism. It stated that

"Moksha is the term used to describe salvation in Hinduism. When an enlightened human being is released from the cycle of life and death (the endless cycle of death and reincarnation), he or she is said to have attained moksha, which is a state of completeness. He then becomes one with God as a result of this experience.

There are four paths that lead to Moksha:

1. The Method of Action: This entails the performance of certain religious ceremonies, duties, and rites, among other things. The goal is to carry out works without regard for personal gain or gain from others.
2. The Path of Knowledge: This path necessitates the application of logic and philosophy in order to achieve a complete understanding of the universe.
3. The Path of Devotion: Salvation is obtained through acts of worship that are motivated by a deep affection for a deity (there are thousands of gods in Hinduism).

The use of meditation and yoga techniques is part of the Royal Road strategy. In most cases, wandering monks are the only ones who employ this method of attaining salvation.

To be saved in Hinduism, a person must follow a specific path that includes a number of requirements. Salvation depends on a person's actions. It is a result of human efforts."

I wasn't doing a single thing properly, or with my whole heart, because of these events. After reading a few books, I realised that I had been given incorrect information about how to find salvation. After a while, I began to spend my remaining free time in the library solely because I needed to understand the purpose of this establishment, but at the same time, I prayed to God to take my life within that time frame. After learning so much about human life from the Vedas, I decided to learn more about the afterlife of my soul by reading about it.

"The Bhagavad-Gita describes two paths along which souls travel after death. One is the path of the sun, also known as the bright path or the path of gods, and the other is the path of the moon, also known as the dark path and the path of ancestors. When a soul travels along the path of the sun, it never returns again, while those that travel along the path of the moon return again. (8.24). Lord Krishna provides the clue in the following verses:

"Controlling all the openings of the body, with the mind established in the heart, fixing the prana in the self at the top of the head establishing oneself in the Yoga, uttering the monosyllable AUM, which is Brahman, who leaves the body remembering Me, he achieves the highest goal. (8.12-13)

In the same chapter, we are also informed that all worlds including that of Brahma are subject to rebirth, but on reaching him there is no birth.

From it, I got to know the reason why we join hands in front of the rising sun and why we don't do good things after sunset. After reading, I was understanding the meaning of all our actions and some beliefs which my mom used to follow. Everything had a meaning.

With all these factors affecting our death and actions in daily life, there were some parameters on which the fate of an individual upon death depends. Those parameters are:

1. Deeds
2. State of Mind
3. Time of Death
4. Grace of Gods

After knowing so much about death and life and the way to moksha, I diverted myself in finding ways to die according to Hindu Mythology because I wanted to attain moksha in only one way, and that was by leaving my body and traveling to the sun or brighter side. There is no book in which the way of dying was written, because according to them, death is decided by God. No one can die before or after the time that is written.

After spending 7 days grabbing knowledge, my mind still wanted to end my life there. It was the only way to escape from all the problems and never come back to life. According to Hindu beliefs, time and place of death also affects the future of the soul.

To calculate a soul's virtue & sins during its lifetime, a person's death is taken for calculations. Given below are the good times for every person to die.

1. Death should occur between Sunrise and Sunset, during the daytime.

2. Death should occur on the floor, not in bed.

3. Death should occur during the peak of the day, at around Noon.

4. Death should occur during the Uthirayanam period (the time, when the Sun starts to travel in the Northern direction) between January 15th to July 14th (approx). Tamil Month (Thai to Ani).

5. Death should occur between the day that comes after New Moon Day to the next Full Moon Day.

6. Days with Thiruthiyai and Ekadesi.

7. Death should not occur on Avittam, Sathayam, Purattathi and Uthirattathi Star.

If a person dies at the above-mentioned time, it indicates that he/she has a lot of virtues to their credit. On the other hand, if a person's death carries "No" to most of the above points, then he/she would have a lot of sins to their credit. According to my calculations, the 15th day of my stay was the only day which fulfilled all the requirements of dying in a good time. But I was ready to die at any point of time in that Bhawan.

After that, I brought some change in my schedule and habits and focused more on setting up the bed for my body. On the 10th day, I got a fever of around 100-101 and started feeling tired. For the last 10 days, I slept around 3-4 hours a day and ate 1-1.5 proper meals on a daily basis. But still I went to the cremation ground to chop the wood, I was near my goal and left with only 45-48 kg of wood. I was happy when I got a fever because it may have been the beginning of my last days. On the 11th day, I finished cutting the wood required to burn my body and prepared a bed for myself. I think I was the first person on this planet who was planning and doing things to die without committing suicide. After completing the task, I filled the form of my death certificate and mentioned the number of my bed on it so that they can know where to cremate me after my death, and from where they have to collect the ashes.

I didn't take any medicine even a single day and my fever was rising. On the 14th day, I recorded a fever of 103.9 degree Celsius. With this temperature, it was difficult for me to move. I had a feeling of dread because I was left with only 36 hours and I didn't want to fail a second time. On the other hand, there were things in my mind which I wanted to do or write before I die.

"The end whispers softly, but it's the waiting, heavy and silent, that lingers in our hearts the longest."

Chapter 14

Cremation

It was the 14th day in Mumukshu Bhawan and in those 14 days, it was the first day when my body was not allowing me to wake up and do my daily tasks. I used the energy from lipids which is a reservoir of energy for the human body. I was really confused because I saw many people dying there and 80% of them had high fever on the last day and hence, I felt that my time had come. It was a weird feeling altogether. For the last few months, I only dreamt of dying, and in the last 14 days, I prepared everything for my cremation rituals. I read a lot of mythological books to understand the meaning and purpose of death and I wanted to know the journey of my soul after death so I read one separate book for that. I was at the final stage of my goal for the first time in my life and I was not happy with it. It is easy to think and plan for death but I was not ready to face it. There was a lot of thought in my mind. My body was not allowing me to even open my eyes properly, and thus, I decided to stay in the room.

Somehow, I managed to stand up on my feet and went to the corner of my room where I kept boiled rice and dal last night. It had the worst taste and rice was uncooked. Everything I was doing could be the last. While I was eating my meal, I burst into tears. According to me, death was at the doorstep, and it was waiting for the right time. I wanted to hug my dad once and call Nikith, but I couldn't. After my dad got a heart attack, he used to tell me that I have to handle my mom after his death. But my mom left him first and I was also about to leave him.

That day, I was so emotional that I wanted to start my life again and be back at home. My heart was telling me to give up on death and start a new life, but my mind was telling me to focus on getting salvation from human life.

I took my bag in which I kept my diaries and sat on the floor of my room. I started remembering all the incidents one by one, just like I had told that person in the interview. At every point of my life, there were things that shouldn't have happened. I started relating everything with what I got to know about life and death from people around me, the books I read and the soul of Girdhari ji. I wished I could have read all those books before, especially Bhagavad Gita. Had I done it earlier, I might have not come here to free my soul from the body. I was just continuously crying while reading my past. I realised that I can't even die properly. I am just a failure. I was here on the planet to maintain a balance between success and failure.

Terry Pratchett said, "It is said that your life flashes before your eyes just before you die." That is true, it's called life. I was just reliving my life again from which I was trying to escape for a long time.

As the clock struck 3 p.m., my countdown to leaving the Mumukshu Bhawan started, and I had only 24 hours left. In those 24 hours, I had to leave that place, but it was yet to be decided whether my body will leave it or will it be my soul. I took a pen from room number 123 and tore some pieces of paper from the bag. I wrote four letters: one was for my dad and the rest for my college friends, or you can say, my only friends in life. It was a gratitude letter. I wanted to convey my mental state and convey as to why I did this. When I started a letter for my dad, I didn't have enough words to write. I was a good writer according to other people and writing was the only way I expressed my thoughts properly, but that day it was the toughest task for me. So, I decided to express it through a poem.

"Ye aap kaise kar lete thy Papa
Din raat ek kar ke hamara pet bhartay
Khud raat ko sote nahi aur din mein kaam par chale jate
Ye aap kaise kar lete the papa

Chahe garmi ho ya sardi
Tum roz kaam par jate
Khud fate hue jutay pehen
Mujhe naye dilatay
Ye aap kaise kar lete thy papa.

Thake haaray ghar aate
Ghar aa kar mujhe ghumne le jate
Homework bhi aap hi karvate the
Ye aap kaise kar lete the papa.

Kabhi na choda mera saath
Ungli thamay har dam mere saath
Jab chalkar thak jata tha toh kandhe par baitha lete
Mera sara bojh apne sar utha lete
Ye aap kaise kar lete the papa

Aaj dukh hai ke itna krne ke baad
Apka beta kuch na kar paya
Jab meri baari aayi kuch karne ke
Main haath chod kar ja raha hu
Shayad ab kabhi na lautu
Itni takleefo mein apne mujhe har dam khush rakha
Ye aap kaise kar lete the papa.

Aapne har cheez sahi kari par mai kuch na kar paya
Apni maa ko maar khud bhi marne chala aaya
Jaise aapne sab kar liya aap yeh bhi kr lena
Mere bina apni zindagi puri jee lena
Apni zindagi puri jee lena"

After I finished the letter, tears began to flow from my eyes, and all of the words became blurred as a result of the tears, so I wrote it back and placed it in the box. I went to the reception with a bag containing all of the letters and diaries I had.

"Harish Sir, please take this bag from me," I said.

"Vihaan, you are not looking well? Is the fever still there?" he replied.

"Yes sir. It is my last day here, and tomorrow I will leave this place. I don't know if my time has come or not.

Either this fever is a sign from God or it is due to my poor eating habits and physical stress on my body. I have also packed my bag."

I continued, "Sir, there is a letter in this bag for my dad and friends along with some diaries in which everything is written about my life. If I die by tomorrow, then please hand this to my dad. I have mentioned his contact number on the envelope. If I fail to die, please cremate all my belongings on the death bed which I prepared for myself."

"Ok, Vihaan, I will do that. I think you have achieved a state of nirvana," he said, and asked me to rest.

While I was walking back to my room, I connected all those things which I experienced. After connecting everything, I came to a conclusion.

Today is my last night here at this bhawan, and tomorrow I will leave this place. I don't know what will happen to me tomorrow. But one thing is certain: tomorrow, I will get salvation. If I die by tomorrow, then I will complete the cycle of life and death, and if not, then I will burn my past here and start a new life with no past to affect me.

I'm still not sure which is the true path to salvation: taking my own life or forgiving myself and moving on with my life. I am experiencing a state of calm and coolness in my mind and heart right now. I'm not making any demands. Neither my soul nor I are pleading with God to extricate itself from my body, nor am I pleading with him to bring me back to life so that I can begin a new and better phase of my life. I had my last meal at this establishment, and the uncooked rice today was absolutely delicious. As a result, I'm going to sleep with a clear head. My future is still up in the air, and this could be my last night on this planet.

If you have read my story till the end and have realised what is the real salvation for human beings, then do convey it to others. There are a lot of Vihaans living hopelessly around you. I have turned off my lights and am going to sleep peacefully with no expectations or planning. If you ever find me anywhere, you will know that I have moved ahead in my life. If not, then I would have completed my circle of life.

If at all, any Vihaan is reading this, then I hope that you decide your future with the help of my story, and are free to do what you want. If you ever go to Mumukshu Bhawan in search of salvation like me, speak to the man sitting at the ghats of Ganga. I hope you do see him. He will change your perspective on life.

Good night, everyone.

OM SHANTI!!!